My Christmas Miracle

My Christmas Miracle

BY

TRACY WILSON

http://beautifulpublications.com

Published by
Beautiful Publications LLC
Stratford, CT 06614

This book is a work of fiction. Names, characters, places, and incidents are either products of the author's imagination or are used fictitiously. Any resemblance to actual events or locales or persons, living or dead, is entirely coincidental.

PRINT ISBN: 978-1-7362753-0-6
EBOOK ISBN: 978-1-7362753-1-3

Printed in the United States of America

"I love you so much..." Ryan breathed as he kissed her...

"I love you too..." Cynthia breathed as she kissed him back. Ryan laid her down on the bed and ran his hands up her back as he continued kissing her... "Ryan... don't..." Cynthia breathed as he tried to unfasten her bra...

"Cyn... please... don't you want me?" he breathed as he began kissing her on her neck while feeling her breasts...

"I want to... but..." Ryan propped himself up on his elbow and looked down at her before he spoke...

"Cyn..."

"Yes Ryan?" she answered with tears in her eyes...

"Baby no... don't cry... we don't have to..." he said as he smoothed her hair away from her face...

"I don't wanna lose you..."

"You're not gonna lose me..." he said as he kissed her gently...

"You promise?"

"Where's this coming from?"

"Well..." Cyn turned her head away from him...

"Uh uh – talk to me..." he said as he turned her face to his...

"Okay..." she sighed as she sat up and folded her arms. Ryan sat up beside her...

"Did I do something?"

"Not you..."

"Not me? What does that mean?"

"It's Chip..."

"Chip? Oh hell no – I'll fuckin' kill him!"

"No Ryan – let me explain..."

"Okay – go ahead..."

"Ally and Chip had sex..."

"Oohh..."

"Please don't tell anybody!"

"I won't... but what's this got to do with us?"

"He broke up with her..." Cyn sighed...

"I swear I wish his dick would fall off..." Ryan sighed as Cyn bust out laughing... "What's so funny?"

"That's what Ally said!" Cyn laughed...

"Is that why you won't have sex with me?"

"Yea..." Cyn sighed as she put her head down...

"Cyn..." Ryan whispered as he picked her head up by her chin and kissed her... "I'm not going anywhere..."

"Neither am I..." Cyn said as she got up off the bed and stood in front of him. Ryan was confused until Cyn took off her black turtleneck shirt and tossed it across the room. Ryan sat there and continued looking at her as she unbuttoned her jeans, unzipped them, and let them fall down to her ankles. Ryan's eyes got big and as he got excited, the blood began rushing to his dick and we waited in anticipation... "Cyn... you're beautiful..." he whispered. Cyn didn't respond. She kicked off her jeans, got back on the bed, and laid down on her back... "Are you sure?" Ryan asked...

"I'm sure..." she answered. We were as excited as Ryan was as he took off his shirt because we realized today was the day we would finally be ejaculated... "Let me get a condom..." he whispered as he slid off his jeans and boxers and his dick sprung out...

"Oh my God – you're huge!" Cyn gasped...

"Touch him..." he commanded...

"Okay..." she said as she reached up and held his dick in her hand...

"Your hand feels so good..." he breathed as Cyn massaged his dick...

"Come here..." she said as she tugged on his dick. Ryan lay down beside Cyn and began kissing her as she continued massaging his dick until he got on top of her... "Ryan... wait..."

"I'll take it slow..."he breathed as he spread her legs and began kissing her on her neck...

"Ryan..." she moaned. Ryan took that as his cue to continue and he moved down to her breasts, lifted her bra, and took turns licking and sucking her nipples... "Ryan..." she moaned as he moved his hands under her back and unhooked her bra. Cyn looked up at him as he slid the bra off her and tossed it across the room. When Ryan started to slide her panties down her hips, she gasped...

"Do you want me to stop?"

"No..." she breathed as she arched her back and Ryan slid her panties down to her ankles and took them off...

"She's pretty..." Ryan breathed as he slid down between her legs and began kissing her on her stomach...

"Ryan..." she moaned...

"Ssshhh..." he breathed as he moved down to her vagina and spread her lips... "Hey beautiful..." he whispered before he flicked his tongue on her clit...

"Ooohhh... Ryan..." she moaned as Ryan began licking and sucking... "Ryan... Ryan... Ryan..." she moaned as she grabbed his head and began riding his face... "Ryan... I'm... I'm... I'm cumming!" she moaned as she arched her back and came up off the bed. Ryan held on to her hips as she rode out her orgasm on his face until her orgasm subsided...

"Was it good?" he asked...

"Oh my God – yyyeesss..." she exclaimed...

"I'll be right back – I need to put the condom on..." he said as he started to get up and she pulled him back down on top of her...

"No..." Cyn breathed as she pulled him back down on top of her...

"Cyn... I don't want you to get preg..." Ryan couldn't finish what he was trying to say because Cyn grabbed him by his ass, pushed him inside her, and pulled him into a kiss before he could react... "Oh Cyn..." he moaned as he began thrusting in and out of her...

"Ryan..." she moaned as she held him down on her and breathed into his neck...

"Oh God... you feel so good..."

"Ryan... I'm gonna cum again... Ryan..."

"Cyn... Oh God... I can't hold it... Fuck..."

"Ryan... Cum with me... Huh..."

"On your mark... get set... go!" I yelled as I shot out of my father's penis first...

"Where are we going?"

"What if we get lost?"

"I'm scared!"

"It's so dark!"

"Will there be a light around the egg?"

"How long will it take to get there?"

"Wait for me!"

"Don't leave me!" I swear – I love them – but all this chatter was getting on my one little nerve – not to mention my concentration...

"Everybody listen!" I yelled as I went up into the cervix... "Follow my voice!" I yelled as I continued towards the lining of the uterus towards the fallopian tube... "Your PMCA Protein will help you navigate! (PMCA Protein – Plasma Membrane CA2+ ATPase) – It's abundant in our tails – (aka our flagella membranes) it alters how we wave, and this directs our movement - there it is!" I yelled as the egg released the Attractant...

"Okay – we're coming!" they all said in unison as I swam ahead of them...

I laughed to myself as I thought about how conversations would go if our parents only knew how we interacted with each other before we reached our destination. They had no idea how boring it was inside our father's balls or how confused we were when we were shot down the throat instead of being shot into the vagina. Whenever sperm was shot down the throat we were really confused – imagine going straight down to the bottom of an acid volcano, only to be burned alive before they knew what was happening – or better yet – being spit into a cloth or a toilet! If I had a choice, I'd rather feed Mommy – at least I'd be serving a purpose before

I die, unless Mommy's allergic to semen, which is known as Human Seminal Plasma Hypersensitivity. This could cause a lot of embarrassment along with the following symptoms: pain, itching, redness, swelling, hives, and difficulty breathing. Personally, I believe that no one is really allergic to semen because if that's the case, the same thing would happen in the vagina. I think what's really happening is that the sperm realize they're not where they're supposed to be and those symptoms described are actually the sperm having tantrums as children due when they're angry – LOL!

As far as digesting sperm – we're not as disgusting as a lot of people think. We have nutrients and other components including sugar, sodium, citrate, zinc, chloride, calcium, tractic acid, magnesium, potassium, and urea.

If you hold us in your mouth long enough to taste us, it's not that bad if our dad's diet is high in celery, parsley, wheat grass, cinnamon, nutmeg, pineapples, papayas, or oranges – but if dad's diet is high in garlic, onions, broccoli, cabbage, leafy greens, asparagus, meat and dairy, alcohol, cigarettes, or coffee, we'll taste more bitter than sweet.

We might also be a mood booster or relaxer because we could contain endorphins, estrone, prolactin, oxytocin, thyrotropin-releasing hormones, and serotonin.

I continued swimming along, happy that we didn't have to fight any other sperm because when that happens, we duel to the death and sometimes the sperm that got there first blocks our path and some of us don't make it – but today that wasn't the case – this time it was happening the way God intended – we went into the vagina, up into the cervix, along the lining of the uterus, and we were all headed to the fallopian tube thanks to our PMCA protein...

"We're coming!" they all yelled in unison. It didn't matter though – I was way ahead of them. The fallopian tube pushed the egg towards the uterus, cilia pushed me towards the egg, and they all cheered... "Yeeaaa!" when I attached myself to the egg. As soon as I penetrated the egg, the surface changed so no other sperm could enter. In 24 hours, Mommy will be pregnant with a little girl. My brothers and sisters will live with me for about 5 days. After that, Mommy's white blood cells will chemically degrade them and absorb them into her body and I'll continue to grow until I'm born...

"Are you okay?" Daddy asked...

"Yea..." Mommy sighed...

"You sure?" he asked as he looked into her eyes...

"I'm sure..." she sighed...

"I love you..." he breathed as he pulled her close to him and held her...

"I know..." she sighed...

"Do you love me?" he asked as if he didn't know the answer...

"Yeesss..." she sighed as she snuggled up underneath him and they both fell asleep.

"Good morning..." Mommy yawned as she stretched...

"Good morning..." Daddy sighed...

"Why didn't' you wake me up?"

"You're beautiful when you're sleeping..." he breathed as he kissed her...

"Oh my God – I gotta call my parents – they must be worried sick..."

"I already spoke to them..."

"You did? When?"

"I spoke to your Dad after... you know..."

"After we made love?"

"Yea..."

"What'd he say?"

"I told him we had been studying for an upcoming exam and you said you needed to take a nap..."

"Well why didn'tcha just wake her up?" Mommy said in a voice I didn't recognize...

"Oh my God..." Daddy laughed... "You sound just like your father!"

"Well – what'd he say?"

"He said to let you sleep..."

"Oh wow – I'm shocked..."

"I'm not..." he said as he snuggled down next to Mommy..."

"You're not?"

"Naa... he knows I'm a good guy..." he said as he got on top of Mommy and started kissing her...

"You... sure... are..." Mommy breathed as Daddy moved down to her breasts and started licking and sucking them...

"Oh yea?" he breathed...

"Yea..." Mommy breathed as she arched her back. Daddy spread Mommy's legs and he was making Mommy feel good... "Ryan... Ryan... Ryan..."

"Oh Cyn... Cyn... Cyn..." Mommy and Daddy were both breathing heavy and I wasn't sure what was happening until I saw some fluid come out of Daddy's penis... "Cyn... I'm cumming..."

"Ryan... I'm cumming with you..."

"Uuggh! Uuggh! Uuggh!"

"Oohh... Oohh... Oohh..."

"Uuuggghhh!"

"Aaahhh!" I was kinda scared because Mommy and Daddy got louder and I thought they were hurting each other until Daddy spoke...

"Oh Cyn... you make me feel so good..."

"You make me feel good too Ryan..."

"Hiiii!" I heard and when I looked down I saw my brothers and sisters...

"Aww... Hiii!" I beamed. I was so happy I must've started secreting endorphins and serotonin because Mommy got really emotional...

"Cyn... what's wrong?"

"I'm so happy..."

"I'm happy too... but..."

"But what?"

"Sigh... we didn't use a condom..."

"I know..."

"What if you're pregnant?"

"What if I am?"

"You are Mommy!" I yelled...

"Cyn – I love you – but we should've been more responsible..."

"I thought that's what you wanted..." Mommy sighed...

"You thought that's what I wanted?"

"I thought we were just going to have sex but..."

"Ooohhh..."

"You're the only one that's ever touched me there... or anywhere..."

"I know..."

"You know?"

"I knew you were a virgin... and... I have a confession to make..."

"You do?"

"I've never done that before..."

"Never?"

"Never..."

"Why not?"

"I wanted to wait until I fell in love..."

"Oh Ryan... I love you too – that's why I didn't want to use a condom..."

"So... you wanted to get pregnant?"

"I just wanted to make you feel as good as you made me feel..." she sighed...

"It's funny – my Dad always told me to make sure I use a condom – but he never used any!"

"Oh my God – is that how you got here?"

"I think so..."

"I'm sorry..."

"I'm not – when you pulled me inside you the way you did... I was in heaven..."

"So was I..."

"What are we gonna do if you're pregnant? We're still in high school!"

"Your parents made it work – didn't they?"

"I guess..."

"We'll make it work too..."

"How Cyn?"

"We don't even know if I'm pregnant – but if I am – we'll graduate in June – I won't be showing until September..."

"How can you be so calm? What about college?" I started getting anxious as Daddy raised his voice...

"I'm sorry Ryan... If I'm pregnant I won't have the baby..."

"Oh yes you will!"

"You mean it?"

"Hell yea – my Dad figured it out – I'll figure it out too..."

"We'll figure it out..." Mommy said as she snuggled up to Daddy...

"I wonder if this is how it happened with my parents..."

"I wonder if your father did to your mother what you did to me..."

"He did..."

"He did? Oh my God! How do you know?"

"I saw him..."

"You saw him?"

"One night I couldn't sleep and I heard my mother moaning so I got up and went to their room – I opened the door – and I saw my Dad eating my Mom..."

"Oh my God! I can't believe it! I would've run away screaming!"

"I was 12 years old at the time – I didn't really know what sex was – I didn't think they were having sex – I really thought he was eating my mother..." he laughed...

"You weren't scared?"

"Yea – I was scared..."

"What'd you do?"

"I watched them and I heard my mother say don't stop – I ran upstairs to my room and cried..."

"Aww..."

"I was so happy to see my mother when I woke up..."

"Oh my God – did you ever tell your parents about that?"

"Never – you're the only person I've ever told..."

"Really? You never told Chip?"

"Chip? Oh please – I'd never tell him anything – especially that!"

"I thought all the guys talked about sex..."

"We do – but Chip does more bragging and gossiping than anything else – I thought he was a virgin until you told me he had sex with Ally..."

"And then he broke up with her..."

"Typical jerk – Ally could be the one – and he'll never know because he does what he always does..."

"Can I ask you something?"

"Sure..."

"Why are you friends with him?"

"I'm not really his friend..."

"You're not?"

"I like Chip – but we only see each other on the court – he doesn't bother with me when we don't have a game..."

"That sucks..."

"It doesn't bother me – I'm not interested in drinking and partying every night – I don't know how he does it – oh wait – I forgot – yes I do..."

"How does he do it?"

"I can't tell you..."

"Fine then – don't tell me..."

"He has somebody do his papers for him..."

"Did he ever ask you to do his papers?"

"He asked – I said no – he never asked again – I hope he doesn't get into Harvard..."

"You're going to Harvard?"

"Yea..."

"Oh my God! Why didn't you tell me?"

"I was going to tell you yesterday... but..."

"Oh I see – so it's my fault huh?" Mommy laughed...

"Yes it is..." Daddy laughed...

"Sigh... I hope I can still go to college..."

"What?"

"If I'm pregnant..."

"My mom went to college when she was pregnant with me..."

"She did?"

"She sure did – she told me she didn't let me stop her – she let me motivate her..."

"Aww..."

"What's college?" I asked as if they could hear me...

"I love you – and if you're pregnant..." he said as he slid down Mommy's body to her stomach... “I love you too...” he said as he kissed Mommy’s stomach...

“I love you too...” Mommy and I said in unison...

"Good morning Mother..." Daddy said as he walked in...

"Good morning – you're just in time for breakfast..." his mother said as she went up to him and gave him a quick hug... "Your father's in the dining room..."

"Thanks Mom..." he said as she turned to go back into the kitchen and he went into the dining room... "Good morning Dad..."

"Morning..." his father said as he took a sip of coffee and continued reading the paper without looking up...

"Breakfast is ready..." his mother said as she brought in a tray of scrambled eggs and a tray of bacon and set them on the table...

"Thank you Dear..." his father said...

"Honey – you don't have to thank me..." she said...

"I don't thank you because I have to – I thank you because I love you and I appreciate you..."

"Oh Ryan..." she gushed...

"Ummm – do you need me to help you with anything Mom?" Daddy asked...

"No Ryan – thanks..." she answered as she went back into the kitchen...

"Son... you and I need to talk..."

"Leave him alone Ryan..." his mother laughed as she came back into the dining room with a tray of toast, butter, jelly, another pot of coffee, and put it on the table...

"I'll get that..." his father said as he got up and pulled out the chair for Ryan's mother to sit down...

"Thank you Dear..." she said as she sat down...

"You're welcome Dear..." Ryan's father said as he pushed her chair in and then he went to sit back down...

"So Ryan – how's Cynthia?" his mother asked as she took some eggs off the plate and passed it down...

"She's fine..." Daddy sighed...

"I bet she is..." Ryan's father said as he took some eggs off the plate and passed it to Ryan...

"You sure are spending a lot of time together..." his mother said as she took some bacon off the plate and passed it down...

"I agree – he has been spending a lot of time with Cynthia..." his father said as he took some bacon off the plate and passed it down...

"I'm sorry Mom – I don't mean to neglect you..." Daddy said as he took some bacon off the plate...

"Don't be sorry – I'm happy for you..." his mother said as she took some toast, buttered it, and added jelly...

"Thanks Mom..." Daddy said as he took some toast, buttered it, and added jelly...

"Do you love her?" his father asked as he took some toast, buttered it, and added jelly...

"Yea..." Daddy sighed...

"Oh Ryan – that's wonderful!" his mother exclaimed...

"I'm happy for you son..." his father said...

"Thanks Dad..."

"We'll finish breakfast – and then we need to talk..."

"Leave him alone Ryan..." his mother laughed...

"Joshy – Ryan's not a little boy anymore – he's a man..."

"Don't pay your father any mind – you'll always be my baby..." Joshy said...

"I know Mom..." Daddy acknowledged. They all sat at the table and continued eating.

The only noise that could be heard was the clanging of the forks on the plates and the occasional stirring of coffee when they added sugar or cream...

"Good morning..." Mommy said as she walked in...

"I bet it is..." her father said as he walked up to her and pulled her into a hug...

"Hi Daddy..."

"How's my girl?"

"I'm fine Daddy..."

"Cyn – you're home – good – I made pancakes..." her mother said as she took Mommy by the hand and pulled her into the kitchen...

"Okay, okay – I'm coming!" Mommy laughed. Her father followed them both into the kitchen. Mommy's mother went over to the stove, put the pancakes on the plate, brought the plate to the table, and put the plate on the table. Mommy sat down, her father sat down, and started asking questions...

"So what were you studying?"

"Huh?" Mommy answered...

"Last night – Ryan called and said you needed to take a break from studying – what were you studying?"

"Chemistry..." Mommy answered...

"Is that right?" her father asked, raising an eyebrow...

"Yea – I'll be glad when I graduate – I can't stand chemistry!" Mommy said...

"Let's eat..." her mother said as she sat down and took some pancakes...

"Thanks Mom – I'm hungry..." Mommy said as she took some pancakes...

"Thank you Bri..." her father said...

"You're welcome Robert..." Bri said...

"So are you changing your major?" Robert asked as he poured out the syrup...

"Yes – I'm going with Business Administration..."

"Are you sure you wanna do that Cyn?" Bri asked... "You'd make a lot more money as a nurse..."

"I know..." Mommy answered as she poured some syrup on her pancakes... "But I've decided I don't wanna be a nurse..."

"Since when?" Robert asked...

"Since Covid 19..."

"Oh Cyn – don't let that stop you..." Bri said...

"It's not just that Mommy – I saw how hard they worked, I saw what they went through – it changed them Mommy – I don't think I can deal with that...

"You're stronger than you think – you have a good heart – you're compassionate – the world could use more nurses like you..."

"Thank you Mommy – but I don't wanna be a nurse anymore..."

"Are you sure?" Robert asked...

"I'm sure Daddy..."

"Okay – as long as you're still going to college you can do whatever you want..." he said as he got up from the table, walked over to her, and kissed her on her forehead...

"Thank you Daddy..."

"I won't pretend I'm not disappointed – I was imagining you as a nurse – but I agree with your father – as long as you go to college you can be whatever you want..."

"Thank you Mommy..." Bri got up from the table and started collecting the plates but Robert stopped her...

"Honey – le'me get the dishes – this way you can go talk to Cyn and make sure she understands chemistry..." Robert said as he took the plates from her...

"Umm... okay – c'mon Cyn – let's go upstairs..."

"Okay Mommy..." When they got upstairs, Mommy thought she was going to lie down...

"We need to talk..." Bri said as she pushed Mommy into the room and closed the door behind them...

"Mommy – what's wrong?" my mother asked as she sat down on the bed...

"Do you have something you need to tell me?"

"No Mommy..."

"Do you have something you want to tell me?"

"No Mommy..."

"Sigh... well... I have something I wanna ask you..."

"Umm... okay..."

"Do you love Ryan?"

"Yea..."

"I love your father too..."

"I know that Mommy..."

"And when I was younger... I fell asleep studying chemistry too..."

"Really?"

"Yes... and after your father made love to me for the first time, our chemistry changed..."

"Oh my God – Mommy – I..."

"Cyn..." she said as she took Mommy's hand... "You can tell me... if you want..."

"Okay..." Mommy sighed...

"I knew it!"

"How?"

"You have the glow..."

"I'm glowing?"

"Yes..."

"Does Daddy know?"

"Why else would he tell me I need to make sure you understand chemistry?"

"Oh my God!" Mommy laughed...

"So was it everything you dreamed of?"

"Yea..." Mommy sighed...

"I remember the first time your father made love to me like it was yesterday...." she sighed...

"Aww... you're smiling... that means Daddy made you happy..."

"Yes he did..."

"Can I ask you something?"

"Sure..."

"Were you nervous?"

"Oh yea..."

"I was nervous too..."

"Do you wanna ask me anything else?"

"No Mommy – that's okay..." my mother laughed...

"Son – come with me..." Ryan said as he got up from the table...

"Where are we going?"

"Joshy – we'll be in the library..."

"Okay Dear..." When they got in the library Ryan closed the door...

"Sit down son..."

"Dad – what's wrong?"

"You love Cyn?"

"Yes Dad..."

"Are you seeing anyone else?"

"No Dad..."

"That's good – once I met your mother I didn't see anyone else either – I didn't want anyone but her..."

"That's how I feel about Cyn..."

"Have you taken your relationship to the next level?"

"Dad... I don't wanna talk about this..."

"I didn't wanna talk about it either..."

"Really? Why?"

"I was embarrassed..."

"You? Embarrassed?"

"Yes me – embarrassed – I was 18 years old – I was on top of the world – I was in love with your mother – and I was embarrassed to talk to my father about it..."

"I made love to her..." Ryan sighed...

"I'm happy for you..."

"I'm happy too..."

"I remember the first time I made love to your mother..."

"I know..."

"How do you know son?"

"Because I'm never going to forget it..."

"No son – you won't..."

"I had no idea it was so beautiful..."

"Really?"

"The guys talk – but they just brag about getting some..."

"That's because they're only interested in sex – they're not interested in love – but that's the difference between us and them – we waited for the one..."

"Were you a virgin when you met Mom?"

"No – but I didn't have sex with every girl that crossed my path..."

"I wasn't a virgin either..."
"Did you remember to use protection?"
"I had protection... but..."
"You didn't use it..." his father sighed...
"I tried to Dad – but..."
"I know – I had it too..."
"Really?"
"Really..."
"If you could go back and do it again..."
"I'd do it again..."
"Me too Dad..."

"Hello?" Mommy yawned as she answered her phone...

"Did I wake you?" Daddy asked...

"Yea..." Mommy answered as she stretched...

"I wish I could take a nap..."

"Why can't you?"

"I had a talk with my Dad..."

"Oh boy..."

"It wasn't as bad as I thought... but I can't stop thinking about it..."

"My Mom had a talk with me too..."

"Really?"

"Yea – my father told her she needed to make sure I understood chemistry..." Mommy laughed...

"Oh shit – you had it worse than I did!" Daddy laughed...

"Did your father ask you what happened?"

"I'm pretty sure he knew what happened..." Daddy laughed...

"That's not what I mean..."

"He asked me if I love you..."

"Aww..."

"He also asked me if I was seeing anybody else..."

"Oh my God!"

"Cyn! You know I'm not seeing anybody else!"

"I know..." Mommy sighed...

"You sure?"

"Yea..."

"So what did your mother ask you?"

"She asked me if I had anything I needed to tell her and I said no..."

"So you didn't tell her?"

"Not right away..."

"So you did tell her..."

"She asked me if I had something I wanted to tell her and I said no..."

"You didn't want to tell her?"

"Not right away..."

"So how did she find out?"

"She asked me if I love you..."

"Aww..."

"And then she told me that when her parents asked her what she was doing, she said she was studying chemistry too..."

"Oh my God!" Daddy laughed...

"She told me about the first time my father made love to her... and she was smiling..."

"Aww... your father made her happy..."

"That's what I said..."

"My father asked me if we took our relationship to the next level..."

"Ooohhh..."

"I told him I didn't wanna talk about that – and guess what he said?"

"What?"

"He said he didn't want to talk about it either..."

"Really? Why?"

"He said he was embarrassed..."

"Oh wow!"

"I know – I couldn't believe it either – he said he was on top of the world, he was in love with my mother, and he was embarrassed to talk to his father... so I told him I made love to you..."

"You told him you made love to me?"

"Yea – does that bother you?"

"No – I just thought you'd tell him we had sex..."

"It was more than sex..."

"My mother said after my father made love to her for the first time, their chemistry changed... so I told her... and she said she knew it..."

"Really?"

"Yea – she said I was glowing..."

"Aww..."

"I asked her if she was nervous..."

"Was she?"

"Yea..."

"My father asked me if we used protection..."

"What'd you say?"

"I told him I tried to but..."

"So you blamed me?"

"No Cyn – my father cut me off before I could finish..."

"My mother asked me did I want to ask her anything else – I said no – that's okay..." Mommy laughed...

"Why'd you tell her no?"

"I didn't want her asking me anything else!" Mommy laughed...

"I asked my father if he could do it all over again – he interrupted me and said he would do it again... and I told him I'd do it again too..."

"Well... technically... you did..." Mommy laughed...

Over the next few months Mommy and Daddy were inseparable. I got used to Mommy and Daddy's moaning and breathing when they were having sex, but every once in a while I'd be a little cranky when I was sleeping and when I got cranky, Mommy would get nauseous and run to the bathroom...

"You okay?" Daddy asked...
"I'm okay..."
"Cyn?"
"Yes Ryan?
"Are you pregnant?"
"I don't know..."
"I think you're pregnant..."
"I think I'm pregnant too..."
"Come here Cyn..." Daddy said as he patted the bed for her to sit. Mommy sat down next to Daddy and he put his arm around her... "We need to find out if you're pregnant..."
"I know..."
"I bought a pregnancy test..."
"You did?"
"Yea..."
"I bought one too..."
"I guess you didn't take it..."
"No..."
"Why?"
"I keep thinking about my parents..."
"Your parents?"
"They'll be so disappointed..."
"Maybe not..."
"You don't know my parents..."
"Yes I do..."

"My Dad is worse than my Mom..." Daddy got up off the bed, went over to his desk, and took the pregnancy test out the drawer...

"Here..."

"You want me to take it now?"

"Yea..."

"Okay..." Mommy sighed as she stood up and took the test from him... "I'll be right back..." she said and then she went into the bathroom and closed the door. Daddy sat on the bed and started shaking his leg as he was listening to Mommy pee...

"How's it going?"

"I'll be out in a minute..." Mommy said as she flushed the toilet. Daddy continued shaking his leg as Mommy turned on the water and washed her hands. When she was done, she opened the door and Daddy stood up...

"Well?"

"We have to wait two minutes..." Mommy said as she walked over to Daddy and they held each other...

"Oh my God – this is crazy – c'mon – let's go look at it!" Daddy exclaimed...

"Okay, okay!" Mommy exclaimed as she hurried into the bathroom...

"Well? Are you pregnant?" Mommy came out the bathroom with the stick behind her back and walked over to Daddy...

"See for yourself..." she said as she handed the stick to him...

"Oh my God... you're pregnant..."

"Yea..." Mommy said as she started to cry...

"Cyn – no – don't cry..." Daddy said as he kissed her eyes and her mouth...

"So you're happy?"

"Yes... I'm happy..."

"I love you so much..."

"I love you too..." Daddy breathed as he kissed her... "And I love you too..." Daddy said as he bent down and kissed Mommy's stomach...

"We need to tell our parents..." Daddy said...

"I know..." Mommy sighed...

"We can do it together..."

"We can?"

"Sure we can – we'll invite your parents over for dinner – and then we'll tell them together...

"My father is going to be mad at both of us..." Mommy sighed...

"I can handle your Dad..."

"I dunno about that..."

"Listen to me..." Daddy said as he turned Mommy around to face him... "I love you..." he breathed as he kissed her... "We're having a baby..." he breathed as he kissed her again...

"And there's nothing your father can do about it..."

"I love you too... but... I'm scared..." Mommy sighed...

"Is your father going to hurt me?"

"Oh no – he'll just yell about how irresponsible we are..."

"Is that what you're afraid of?"

"I just don't want to disappoint him..."

"I'll be right there with you..."

"Okay..."

"Okay – we need to check out – I need to get home – I have a few errands to run – and I need to speak to your father before we invite your parents over for dinner..."

"You need to speak to my father? Why?"

"You'll find out soon enough – but I need you to do something for me..."

"What?"

"I need you to look into Harvard's online classes..."

"I can go to school while I'm pregnant..."

"In the beginning you can – once you start showing you might not fit in the seat..." Daddy laughed...

"I forgot about that..." Mommy laughed...

"Okay – let's do this..." Daddy said as he took Mommy's hand and pulled her out the door...

"Are you checking out?" the clerk asked...

"Yes we are..." Daddy answered as he put the key on the counter...

"Okay – I'll just print you out a receipt..." she said...

"Here ya go – thank you for being our customer..."

"You're welcome – c'mon Cyn!" Daddy exclaimed as he pulled Mommy by the hand...

"Okay, okay!" Mommy laughed...

"I'm sorry – I can't help it – I'm so excited!"

"I'm glad you're excited..." Mommy sighed as Daddy opened the door and she got in the car. Daddy went over to the driver's side, opened the door, got in the car, and took Mommy's hand...

"We're gonna be okay – I promise..." he said as he kissed Mommy's hand. Mommy didn't say anything. Daddy started the car, left the parking lot, and neither one of them said anything until Daddy pulled up in front of Mommy's house... "You okay Cyn?"

"Yea..."

"Come here..." Daddy breathed as he pulled Mommy into a kiss...

"I love you Ryan..."

'I love you too – I'll call you later..."

"Okay..." Mommy said as she got out of the car...

"Hi Mommy..." my mother said as she walked into the house...

"Hi Cyn – you hungry?"

"Yea..."

"What's a matter with that boy?" Robert asked as he walked into the kitchen...

"Good morning Daddy..."

"Good morning – why doesn't Ryan feed you?"

"He said he had some errands to run..." Mommy said as Bri put plates of bacon, scrambled eggs, and potatoes on the table... "Thank you Mommy..."my mother said as she started eating...

"So what's Ryan up to?" Bri asked as she sat down and started eating...

"He didn't tell me..."

"So Ryan just dropped you off without saying anything? Okay that's it – I'ma have to sit him down and have a serious conversation..."

"He's coming to talk to you later..."

"Is that right?"

"Yea – he told me he had some errands to run, and then he wants to come talk to you..." Mommy said as she got up from the table... "I'm getting juice – you want some?"

"Sure Cyn – I'll have some..." Bri said...

"Okay – you want some Daddy?"

"Sure Cyn..."

"Okay – coming right up!" Mommy beamed. Mommy's parents looked at her and they looked at each other. Mommy put two glasses of orange juice on the table and then she poured some for herself... "I'm going upstairs – I have some work I need to finish..." she said as she closed the refrigerator and left her parents in the kitchen...

"What was that about?" Bri asked...

"It's either one of two things..." Robert said and then he took a sip of juice... "She's pregnant – or he wants to marry her – and if she's pregnant – he better marry her!"

"Robert..."

"Don't you Robert me – I said what I said!"

"Ryan – you're home!" Joshy exclaimed as she pulled him into the house and hugged him tight...

"Good morning Mom..."

"Good morning Ryan – have you had breakfast?" Ryan asked...

"Good morning Dad – no – I haven't had breakfast yet..."

"You're just in time – I've got scrambled eggs, bacon, potatoes, biscuits, and coffee..." Joshy said...

"Oh my God – that sounds delicious!" Daddy exclaimed as they all went into the dining room and sat down...

"Mom! This is beautiful! What's the occasion?" Daddy asked as he sat down...

"That would be me..." Ryan whispered as he winked...

"Oh my God – Dad!"

"What'd your father do now?" Joshy asked...

"Nothing – Mom... Dad... I have something I need to tell you..." he said as they started eating...

"What is it son?" Ryan asked...

"Sigh... I'm going to talk to Cyn's father later today..."

"Oh Ryan! Does this mean what I think it means?" Joshy asked...

"Yes..."

"Oh Ryan! Congratulations!" Joshy said as she got up, ran over to Daddy, and started hugging and kissing him...

"Joshy – let him breathe!" Ryan laughed...

"I can't help it – I'm so happy – I love Cyn – I love you..."

"Congratulations son..." Ryan said as he got up to hug Daddy...

"Thanks Dad..."

"I'll get the ring for you..."

"No Dad – wait..."

"Wait?"

"Yes – I told Cyn I wanted to invite her parents over for dinner..."

"You want to propose to her here?"

"Yea..."

"Oh Ryan!" Joshy exclaimed as she started crying...

"Is that okay Dad?"

"That's fine son..." Ryan answered...

"When do you want to do this?" Joshy mother asked...

"Sunday..."

"Okay – that gives me about a day to get everything together..."

"Mom – you don't have to go too extreme..."

"Son – let your mother have her moment..." Ryan laughed...

"Listen to your father!" Joshy laughed...

"I love y'all..." Daddy said...

"We love you too – Cyn is a lucky girl..." Ryan said...

"I'm the lucky one Dad..."

"Aww... that's the same thing your father told me..."

"So how do you want to do this?" Ryan asked...

"I want us to have dinner, have dessert, you say you'll be right back, you give me the ring, I get down on bended knee, and then I'll propose..."

"Oh Ryan – I'm so happy – will this be a surprise?" Joshy asked...

"Cyn knows I want us all to have dinner – but she doesn't know I'm going to propose..."

"Oh wow..." Ryan said...

"What time should we do dinner?" Joshy asked...

"If her father's a sports man – he'll wanna watch the game..." Ryan said...

"I'll make dinner at 4pm..." Joshy said...

"Okay – thanks – I need to go talk to Cyn's father – I'll see you later tonight..." Daddy said as he hurried out the door...

"Hello?"

"Hi Cyn..."

"Hi Ryan..."

"I'm on my way..."

"Okay!"

"Cyn?"

"Yes Ryan?"

"I need to talk to your Dad... alone..."

"Are you gonna tell him?"

"No Cyn – we'll tell them on Sunday when we're all having dinner..."

"Sunday?"

"At 4pm – le'me get off the phone while I'm driving – I'll see you soon..." Daddy said and then he hung up...

"Cyn?"

"Yes Mommy?"

"Ryan's here..."

"Okay!" Mommy squealed as she ran downstairs and into his arms...

"Hi Cyn..." Daddy laughed...

"Hello Ryan – come on in..." Bri laughed...

"Is your father here?" Daddy asked...

"He's in the library – I'll go get him..." Mommy said as she went to the library...

"Come sit in the living room..." Bri said as she went towards the living room and Daddy followed...

"Daddy?"

"Yes Cyn?"

"Ryan's here..."

"That's nice – tell him I said hello..."

"He wants to talk to you..."

"Okay..." Robert said as he got up and followed Mommy into the living room...

"Good afternoon..." Daddy said...

"Good afternoon Ryan – Cyn said you wanted to speak to me?" Robert asked as he sat down...

"I'd like you to come over to my parent's house for dinner on Sunday at 4 pm..."

"Oh wow – somebody else cooking for a change – that's fine with me!" Bri laughed...

"That's close to game time..." Robert said...

"My Dad watches the game too..." Daddy said...

"Really? What team?"

"My father like the Patriots..."

"Figures..." Robert laughed...

"Oh boy – my father's gonna love this..." Daddy sighed...

"I'm sure he'll be fine..."

"So you'll come?"

"We'll be there..."

"Good – I'll let my parents know..."

"Okay Ryan..." Robert said as he got up...

"Umm... Mr. Lawrence?"

"Yes Ryan?"

"Can we talk... in private?"

"Sure – we'll be in the library ladies..." Robert said as he went towards the library and Daddy followed...

"Come help me wash these dishes..." Bri said as she got up to go in the kitchen...

"Okay..." Mommy sighed...

"Cyn – he'll live!" Bri laughed...

"Okay Ryan – you wanna talk – let's talk..."

"Well... I need to ask you something..."

"I'm listening..."

"I wanna propose to Cyn on Sunday... if that's okay with you..." Robert didn't say anything. He sat there rubbing his chin, thinking, and smiling... "Mr. Lawrence?"

"Yes Ryan?"

"Do I have your permission?"

"I'll think about it..." Robert laughed...

"Okay..." Daddy sighed...

"Okay? I tell you I'll think about it and you say okay?"

"Umm... yea..."

"Le'me ask you a question..."

"Okay..."

"What would you do if I said no?"

"Well... I love your daughter... she loves me... and I'm going to ask her to marry me on Sunday..."

"Are you telling me you're going to propose whether I like it or not?"

"Naa..."

"So you're not going to propose?"

"Oh I'm going to propose – and you're going to like it..." Daddy laughed...

"Is that right?" Robert laughed...

"Yes it is..." Daddy laughed...

"We'll see you Sunday..." Robert laughed as he got up...

"Okay – I gotta go – see you Sunday – tell Cyn I'll see her later!" Daddy said as he hurried out...

"Hi Daddy – where's Ryan?"

"He said he'll see you later – he has errands..."

"Oh God – you didn't run him outta here Robert – did you?" Bri laughed...

"We'll be there Sunday for dinner..." Robert laughed as he went back into the library...

Mommy was up early... "Well well – this is a surprise..." Bri said as she came into the kitchen...

"I couldn't sleep so I figured I'd help you cook..."

"Okay – who are you and what have you done with my child?" Bri laughed...

"I can't help it..." Mommy laughed...

"Well thanks – I appreciate it – but don't you think you should've started breakfast before you started dessert?"

"Nope – the cake needs time to cool..."

"You made the cake so you could lick the bowl..." Bri laughed...

"Good morning..." Robert said...

"Good morning Daddy – coffee's ready..."

"Smells good – and I see you made cake..."

"And apple pie..." Mommy said as she took it out the oven...

"Oh wow..." Robert father said...

"I wanted to help Mommy with the cooking..."

"Okay – who are you and where's my child?" Robert laughed...

"I made breakfast too..." Mommy said as she took the biscuits out the oven...

"Okay Cyn – what's going on?" Bri asked...

"I just wanted to help you Mommy..."

"Well thank you – I appreciate it..." Bri said as her parents went to sit down. Mommy put the biscuits in a bowl and put the bowl on the table...

"I'll get coffee..." Robert said...

"Sit down Daddy – I'll get it..." Mommy said as she got two mugs, poured two cups, and placed them on the table in front of her parents...

"Thank you Cyn..." Robert said...

"You're welcome Daddy..." Mommy said as she went over to the refrigerator, took out the cream, and put it on the table...

"If I knew going to meet Ryan's parents for dinner would get you to help out like this – I would've gone to meet them a long time ago!" Bri laughed...

"There ya go..." Mommy said as she put a plate of scrambled eggs with cheese and turkey sausage on the table...

"Scrambled eggs – with cheese?" Robert asked...

"Oh – sorry Daddy – I forgot..."

"Don't worry about it – I'll eat 'em..." he said as he took some eggs and turkey sausage off the plate along with a biscuit...

"This sure smells good..." Bri said as she took some eggs and turkey sausage off the plate along with a biscuit...

"Thanks Mommy..." Mommy said as she took some eggs and turkey sausage off the plate along with a biscuit and started eating. Mommy's parents watched her as she ate...

"Hungry eh?" Bri asked...

"Mmm hmmm..." Mommy nodded as she continued eating. Mommy got up, poured herself some coffee, sat at the table, and watched her parents as they finished eating...

"Cyn – you're drinking coffee..." Bri said...

"Uh huh..."

"You never drink coffee..."

"I had a taste for it..." Mommy said as she finished her coffee... "I'll wash the dishes Mommy..."

"Okay – that's it – what's going on?" Bri asked...

"Bri – leave her alone!" Robert laughed... "She's excited – she made dessert – she made coffee – she made breakfast – she wants to wash the dishes – let her be!"

"Okay Robert... I'll let her be..." Bri said as she gave him the side eye. Mommy got up from the table, got the plates and silverware, and put them in the sink...

"I'll leave the cups in case you want some more coffee..." Mommy said as she turned her back to them and started washing the dishes...

"Robert – let's go in the library..." Bri said as she got up and they both left the kitchen...

"I think Cyn is pregnant..." Bri whispered...

"Are you serious?" Robert laughed...

"I've been watching her closely – she's sleeping a lot, she's eating more – and she never drinks coffee!"

"I love you..." Robert laughed as he kissed her...

"Robert – I'm serious..."

"Bri – you don't remember – do you?"

"Remember what?"

"You don't remember how nervous I was?" he laughed...

"You were a nervous wreck!" she laughed...

"This is a big deal for Cyn..."

"You're right..."

"Ya know..." he said as he moved up behind her... "We have some time before we go over there..." he whispered in her ear as he put his arm around her...

"Robert... stop..." she laughed...

"No..." he breathed as he began kissing her on her neck...

"Oh Robert..." she moaned...

"Come upstairs with me..." he said as he took her by the hand and led her upstairs...

"Mom? Dad?" Mommy called... "Hmmm – I guess they went back to bed – I'm tired – I'ma sit here for a minute..." she said as she sat in her father's chair...

"Oh Robert..."

"Bri..."

"Robert... Robert... Robert...

"Bri... Bri... Bri..."

"I'm cumming Robert..." Robert kissed her to muffle her moans so Mommy wouldn't hear them... "Mmmm... Mmmm... Mmmm..."

"Mmmph... Mmmph... Mmmph..."

"Hey..."

"Hi Ryan..."

"You okay?"

"Yea... I'm just tired..."

"You sure you're okay?"

"Yea – I was up early – I couldn't sleep so I made chocolate cake and apple pie for dessert..."

"Oh wow – you didn't have to do that..."

"I wanted to..."

"I know my Mom will appreciate it..."

"I made breakfast too..."

"Oh wow – I wish I was there..."

"I wish you were here too..."

"We'll see each other soon..."

"My Mom started asking questions..."

"Really?"

"Yea – I made eggs with cheese and I drank coffee..."

"What's wrong with that?"

"I forgot my Dad doesn't like cheese in his eggs and I never drink coffee..."

"Ooohhh..."

"Thank God my father told her to leave me along..." Mommy laughed...

"Your mother's a detective..."

"Yes she is..."

"Well she'll know in a few hours – they'll all know..."

"Uh huh..." Mommy yawned...

"You should go take a nap..."

"I will – but I'm gonna sit in the library for a while first..."

"Why?"

"Because if I go upstairs now... I'll hear my parents having sex..." Mommy laughed...

"Are you serious?!"

"Yup..."

"How do you know?"

"They don't go upstairs during the day unless they're having sex..."

"Oh wow – that must be awkward..."

"Not really – if I'm in my room I put my headphones on and do school work – If I don't have any work to do I listen to music or I come downstairs to the library..."

"How can you be so cool about it?"

"Well – right now Daddy's keeping her mind off of me..." Mommy laughed...

"Oh Robert... I love you..." Bri breathed as they kissed...

"I love you too..."

"Let's stay here..."

"We can stay here for a while if you want..."

"I'm gonna celebrate when Cyn moves out..."

"Oh yea?"

"Yea..." Bri breathed as she slid down between Robert's legs...

"Got Damn..." he moaned...

"Ssshhh..." Bri whispered as she continued...

Chapter Seven

"Cyn..."

"Yes Daddy?" Mommy yawned...

"We're about ready to go..."

"Okay – I'm up..." Mommy said as she got up...

"You love Daddy's chair..." he sighed...

"It's comfortable..."

"C'mon – your mother's waiting..." he said as he took her by the hand and led her out the library and out the door...

"Where's Mommy?"

"Your mother's coming..." Robert answered as he opened the door for her and she got in... "I'll be right back..." he said as he went to go get her mother...

"Where's Cyn?"

"She's in the car..."

"I wish we could go back upstairs..."

"We will – tonight..."

"I'm looking forward to it..." Bri said as they came outside...

"Mommy – where's the dessert?" Mommy asked...

"Right beside you..." Bri laughed as Robert opened the door and she got in the car...

"I can't wait for you to meet his parents..." Mommy gushed...

"We know..." Robert laughed as they drove off...

"They're here!" Daddy exclaimed as he ran outside...

"There's Ryan..." Mommy sighed...

"I see..." Bri laughed as Robert parked the car...

"Hi Mrs. Lawrence..." Daddy said as he opened the door for Bri...

"Hello Ryan – thank you..."

"Hi Cyn!" Daddy squealed as he opened the door for Mommy...

"Hi Ryan..." Mommy sighed as she got out and they stood there hugging...

"I guess I'll get dessert..." Robert laughed...

"Oh – sorry Daddy..."

"Go on – I got it..." he laughed. When they got to the door, Joshy opened it...

"Hello Cyn..."

"Hi Mrs. Davis – this is my Mom, Bri – and this is my Dad – Robert..."

"Hello..." they both said in unison...

"Hi – it's nice meeting you – I'm Joshy – c'mon in – this is my husband, Ryan – Ryan, this is Bri and Robert..."

"Nice meeting you – c'mon in..." Ryan said...

"Nice meeting you too – Cyn made dessert..." Robert said as he presented the dessert...

"Thank you Cyn..." Joshy said as she took the cake and the pie...

"I'll bring this in the dining room..."

"C'mon – let's go sit down!" Daddy said as he took Mommy by the hand and pulled her into the living room...

"C'mon Robert – we'll join my wife in the dining room..." Ryan laughed as they followed Joshy into the dining room and sat at the table...

"Joshy you have a lovely home..." Bri said...

"Thank you Bri..." Joshy said as she went towards the kitchen...

"Need any help?" Bri asked...

"Sure..." Joshy answered as Bri followed her into the kitchen...

"Ryan tells me you're a Patriot fan..." Robert said...

"I am – but I'm a fan of football too..." Ryan said...

"So am I – I like to keep up on my competition..."

"Who's your team?"

"49ers..."

"No kidding – I like them too..."

"You like the Cowboys?"

"Please don't tell me you like them Cowboys..."

"Hell no!" Robert laughed...

"Oh thank God – I was worried for a minute..." Ryan laughed...

"Dinner's ready..." Joshy said as she came into the dining room and Bri came in behind her...

"Where should I put this?" Bri asked...

"Anywhere you like..." Joshy answered...

"Okay..." Bri said as she put the tray down, Joshy put her tray down, and they both went back into the kitchen...

"I'm glad we're finally meeting face to face..." Robert said...

"So am I..." Ryan agreed...

"Your son's a nice young man..."

"I feel the same way about your daughter..."

"Oh so you feel my daughter's a nice young man?" Robert asked as they both laughed...

"Here ya go..." Joshy said as she and Bri put two more trays on the table... "Ryan! Cyn! Come eat!"

"I'll get us some plates and silverware..." Joshy said as she went back into the kitchen. Daddy got up and followed Joshy...

"You need any help Mom?"

"Yes – get the pitcher of ice tea – and get some glasses..."

"Okay Mom..." Daddy said as he went in the refrigerator. Joshy came back in the dining room and put the plates and silverware on the table and Daddy put the pitcher of ice tea on the table... "I'll be right back – I'll get the glasses...

"I'll help!" Mommy said...

"C'mon then..." Joshy said as they went into the kitchen...

"They're inseparable..." Bri laughed...

"Yes they are..." Ryan agreed...

"Reminds me of us..." Robert said...

"Oh Robert..." Bri sighed as Joshy, Mommy, and Daddy came into the dining room and put the glasses on the table...

"Okay – help yourselves – we've got baked macaroni & cheese, collard greens, potato salad, and ham..." Joshy said...

"Joshy – thank you – you didn't have to go through all the trouble – but I'm glad you did..." Bri laughed...

"You're welcome – but don't worry – we can have dinner at your house next time..." Joshy laughed...

"I'll cook..." Robert said...

"You can cook?" Ryan asked...

"Oh yea..." Robert said...

"Maybe you can give my husband some lessons..." Joshy laughed...

"Ryan – you don't know how to cook?" Robert asked...

"I'm nobody's chef..." Ryan laughed...

"Dad – I didn't know you couldn't cook..." Daddy said...

"Can you cook Cyn?" Joshy asked...

"I sure can!" Mommy exclaimed...

"Oh well – five that can cook – one that can eat – I'm good!" Ryan said they all laughed. Everybody ate, laughed, and drank until they were good and full – but I was hoping Mommy would want some dessert... and then Daddy spoke...

"Umm... Dad?"

"Yes son?"

"Could you go get that book out the library?"

"You sure?"

"Yea..."

"Okay – I'll be right back..." Ryan said as he got up and went to the library. When he came back into the dining room he handed Daddy a box and then Daddy took Mommy's hand and started to speak...

"Cyn..."

"Yes Ryan?"

"When I was little, my grandmother told me I was going to grow up, fall in love, and get married...

"Oh Ryan..." Mommy said as she started crying...

"She said she wanted me to keep this ring until I met the woman I was going to marry..." Daddy said and then he got down on one knee... "And now that I've found her... now that I've found you... I need to ask you something..." Daddy said as he opened the box... "Cynthia Lawrence..."

"Yes Ryan?"

"Will you marry me?" Mommy waited for Daddy to put the ring on her finger before she answered...

"Yes Ryan... Yes... Yes..." Daddy stood up, pulled Mommy into a hug, and kissed her as the camera's flashed...

"Robert? Did you know about this?" Bri asked...

"I have a confession to make..."

"So you did know!"

"Ryan asked my permission to ask Cyn to marry him on Saturday...

"Oh my God!" Mommy and Bri exclaimed in unison...

"Why didn't you tell me?!" Bri exclaimed...

"Bri – I love you – but we both know you can't hold water!" Robert laughed...

“Welcome to the family Cyn...” Joshy said as she pulled Mommy into a hug...

“Thanks Mom...”

“Welcome to the family son...” Robert said as he pulled Daddy into a hug...

“Thanks Dad...”

“I’m going to be Mrs. Davis...” Mommy said as she looked at the ring on her hand...

“We have an announcement to make...” Daddy said...

“I’m pregnant...” Mommy said...

Nobody said anything. Mommy and Daddy looked at their parents and then they looked at each other and waited for somebody to say something...

"Congratulations..." Joshy said...

"Thanks Mom..." Daddy said...

"Congratulations..." Ryan said...

"Thanks Dad..."

"I guess you were right Bri..." Robert said...

"Yes I was..." Bri said as she smiled...

"You knew I was pregnant?" Mommy asked...

"Yea... I knew..." Bri answered...

"Mr. Lawrence – Dad – I'm gonna do right by Cyn – I..."

"Stop right there..." Robert interrupted... "Don't tell me what you're going to do – show me..."

"I will..." Daddy said...

"Son – remember what I told you..." Joshy said...

"When you were pregnant with me, you didn't let that discourage you – you let that encourage you..." Daddy said...

"That's right..." Joshy said...

"I'm glad you know Mommy..." Mommy said...

"I bet you are..." Bri said...

"Now I don't have to avoid your questions..." Mommy laughed...

"Guess again..." Bri laughed...

"Your mother's just getting started..." Robert laughed...

"Oh boy..." Mommy sighed...

"Anybody ready for dessert?" Ryan asked...

"I am!" I yelled as if they could hear me...

"Let's have dessert..." Joshy said...

"I'll help you..." Bri said as she got up and followed Joshy into the kitchen...

"Congratulations Grandma..." Bri laughed...

"Thanks Grandma..." Joshy laughed...

"They'll be okay..."

"I know..."

"Let's turn it up a bit..." Bri said a she picked up the chocolate cake...

"Okay..." Joshy agreed as she picked up the apple pie and they both went back into the dining room and put dessert on the table...

"That cake looks good..." Daddy said. Bri and Joshy went back into the kitchen to get plates, forks, and cake cutters, came back into the dining room, put the plates, forks, and cake cutters on the table, and sat down...

"So..." Joshy said as she cut a piece of cake... "You'll be graduating soon..."

"Yes Mom..." Daddy said...

"What are your plans after graduation?" Bri asked... as she cut a piece of pie...

"We're still going to college..." Mommy answered...

"Uh huh..." Joshy said as she continued cutting the cake and put a piece on each plate...

"So you're going to bring your baby to class?" Bri asked as she continued cutting the pie and put a piece on each plate...

"I'm going to go to class until I can't fit in the seat anymore – once that happens, I'll take classes online..." Mommy answered as she took a plate of cake, took a plate of pie, and started eating...

"Will you be taking classes online as well?" Ryan asked as he took a plate of cake...

"I plan on going to class as long as I can..." Daddy answered as he took a plate of cake...

"As long as you can? What does that mean?" Robert asked as he took a plate of pie...

"I don't want to leave Cyn alone – I want to be there when she needs me..." Daddy answered...

"Have you thought about where you're going to live?" Joshy asked...

"I was thinking we'd move to Massachusetts..." Daddy answered...

"Do you have a job lined up?" Ryan asked...

"Not yet..." Daddy answered...

"So you plan on applying for a job?" Robert asked as he took a piece of pie...

"Yes..." Daddy answered...

"So where are you going to live in the meantime?" Joshy asked...

"I'm going to continue living here... with you... if that's alright..." Daddy answered...

"Ryan – of course you can live here – but you're getting married – you're having a baby – it's not just about you anymore..." Ryan said...

"I know..." Daddy acknowledged...

"Cyn – you're quiet..." Bri said...

"I'm just thinking..."

"I bet – you have a lot to think about..."

"I didn't know Ryan was going to ask me to marry him..."

"Did you have a plan Cyn?" Robert asked...

"I planned on going to college..."

"Where were you planning on staying?"

"I was planning on staying with you..."

"Ryan – I'm happy you proposed to my daughter – but my question to both of you is this: what now?" Robert asked...

"I thought I could live with my parents until I started college..." Daddy answered...

"When are you due Cyn?" Joshy asked...

"I think I'm due in December... at Christmas..."

"At Christmas? Oh wow – that'll be nice..." Bri said...

"It would be even nicer if we knew where our grandchild would be..." Ryan laughed...

"Exactly..." Robert laughed...

"Have you thought about when you wanna get married?" Joshy asked...

"I'd like to get married before we go to college... if that's alright with you..." Daddy answered as he took Mommy's hand and kissed it...

"That's fine..." Mommy gushed...

"So you plan to marry Cyn before you start college, and then what?" Ryan asked...

"Well..." Daddy sighed... "I was gonna ask you later on... but since we're all here... I'll ask you now..."

"Ask me what?" Ryan asked as he leaned closer to Daddy...

"After we get married – can we live here?"

"I guess so..." Ryan sighed...

"Thanks Dad..." Daddy said as he hugged Ryan...

"Cyn?" Bri asked...

"Yes Mommy?"

"Is that what you want?" Joshy looked at Bri in surprise for asking...

"As long as I'm with Ryan... I don't care where we live..." Mommy sighed...

"You could live with us too..." Robert said...

"We can?" Mommy asked...

"Of course you can..." Robert answered as he hugged Mommy...

"I don't know what I wanna do now..." Mommy laughed...

"You don't have to decide right this minute..." Bri said...

"We can talk about this more next week when you come to our house for dinner..." Robert said...

"Okay..." Ryan agreed...

"Getting' close to game time..." Robert said as he stood up...

"You're right – let's go..." Ryan said as he got up and they both left the dining room...

"Well..." Joshy said as she got up..." I might as well get started on the dishes...

"Mom – relax – I'll do the dishes..." Daddy said...

"C'mon Bri..." Joshy said as she got up...

"I'm right behind you..." Bri said as she got up and they left the dining room...

"You okay?" Daddy asked as he pulled Mommy into a hug...

"Yea..." Mommy sighed...

"I hope you're not upset with me – I was gonna talk to you later about getting married and moving in with my parents...

"They didn't really give you a chance..." Mommy laughed...

"So you're not upset with me?" Daddy asked as he turned on the water and added the soap...

"I'm not upset... I'm happy..." Mommy sighed...

"I love you so much..."

"I love you too... Ryan – look out!" Mommy exclaimed...

"Ooops..." Daddy laughed as he turned off the water before it ran onto the floor...

"Let some of that out..." Mommy said as she filled the other sink with water and got a towel. Daddy let some of the water out, and then he started washing the dishes and passing them to Mommy so she could dry them... "Ryan?"

"Yes Cyn?"

"Did you ask me to marry you because I'm pregnant?"

"Cyn... look at me..." Daddy said as he stopped washing the dishes and turned Mommy to face him...

"Yes Ryan?"

"What did I tell you when I proposed?"

"You said your grandmother told you to keep the ring until you found the girl you wanted to marry..."

"Okay then..." Daddy said and then they went back to washing and drying the dishes...

"Ryan?"

"Yes Cyn?"

"Where do you sleep?"

"In my room..." Daddy laughed...

"I know that..." Mommy laughed... "I mean do you sleep upstairs or downstairs..."

"Downstairs..."

"Oh good – you don't have to hear your parents having sex..." Mommy laughed...

"Oh yes I do..." Daddy laughed...

"You do?"

"Yea..." Daddy laughed... "Mom's a screamer..."

"Oh my God!" Mommy laughed... "What if... Never mind... Forget it..."

"What if you scream?"

"Yea..."

"You won't – you'll be too busy trying not to get caught..." Daddy laughed...

"Do you think our baby hears us having sex?"

"Of course!"

"Oh my God – poor baby..." Mommy laughed...

"I'm sure we heard our parent's having sex before we were born too..." Daddy laughed...

"I sleep upstairs..."

"I know – you told me..."

"What if my parents have sex when we're having sex?"

"Oh my God – I don't even wanna think about that!" Daddy laughed...

"I wish we didn't have to live with anybody!" Mommy laughed...

"It'll just be until the baby is born..."

"You want us to live with our parents until Christmas?"

"The longer we live with our parents, the more money we can save – plus, our parents can help with the baby..."

"I don't know..." Mommy sighed...

"You don't wanna live with our parents?"

"I thought we were just gonna live with them until we started college..."

"So you wanna move to Massachusetts?"

"Yea..."

"We can do that..."

"You're not mad?"

"Cyn... I love you – I want you to be happy..."

"I want you to be happy too..."

"Let's wait until after we have dinner next week before we decide what we're gonna do..."

'Okay – but I still wanna get married after we graduate..."

"Me too..."

"Those poor kids are traumatized..." Joshy laughed...

"If they're traumatized now – wait until the baby comes!" Bri laughed...

"They wanna be grown – they gotta take what comes with it..." Joshy sighed...

"Absolutely..." Bri agreed...

"I'm just happy Ryan picked a good girl to settle down with..."

"Aww... thank you for saying that..."

"You're welcome – she's really sweet..."

"I'm happy Cyn is marrying your son too..."

"Good..."

"Next week should be interesting..." Bri laughed...

"I can't wait..." Joshy laughed...

"I hope Ryan's ready for this..." Ryan sighed...

"He's ready..." Robert said...

"You think so?"

"I know so..."

"What makes you so sure?"

"He answered every question that was thrown at him..."

"True – but he still needs to come up with a definite plan..."

"That's where we come in..."

"We?"

"Your son came to me as a man and told me he wanted to ask my daughter to marry him if it was okay with me..."

"What if it wasn't okay?" Ryan laughed...

"I told him I would think about it and he said okay..." Robert laughed...

"He said okay?"

"He said okay – and I asked him what he'd do if I said no..."

"What'd he say?"

"He said he loves my daughter, he's going to ask her to marry him, and I'm gonna like it..." Robert laughed...

"Hot Damn!" Ryan exclaimed...

"He's a good man..."

"Thank you for saying that..."

"C'mon – I'll show you my room..." Daddy said as he took Mommy by the hand and pulled her into the living room...

"Where are you two going?" Joshy asked...

"I'm showing her my room..." Daddy answered as he pulled Mommy towards his room before his mother could ask any more questions...

"You have a nice room..." Mommy said as she sat down on the bed and started bouncing up and down...

"What are you doing?"

"I wanna see if it squeaks..." Mommy laughed...

"I guess we better head on home..." Robert said as he got up...

"You sure?"

"Are you asking me to stay?" Robert laughed...

"Naa... You'll be here soon enough..." Ryan laughed...

"Fuck you then..." Robert laughed...

"Fuck you too..." Ryan laughed... as they left the library and went into the living room...

"Where'd they go?" Robert asked...

"They're in his room..." Joshy answered...

"Watch this..." Ryan said as he stormed towards Ryan's room with Robert right behind him. When they got to Ryan's room, his dad banged on the door really hard...

"Who is it?" Daddy asked...

"Y'all ain't married yet – open this got damned door!"

"Okay Dad – sorry!" Daddy said as he hurried up to open the door...

"Aaaahhh Haaa Haaa Haaa!" Ryan and Robert laughed in unison...

"Really Dad?" Daddy asked...

"What happened?" Joshy said as she came running with Bri close behind...

"Just having a lil' fun..." Ryan laughed...

"What's a matter Cyn? Not funny?" Bri asked...

"Not really..." Cyn answered as she rolled her eyes...

"We're gonna get ready to go..." Robert said...

"Okay Dear – it was really nice meeting you Joshy..." Bri said as she hugged her...

"Nice meeting you too..." Joshy said as she hugged Bri back...

"I'll see you next week..." Robert said as he gave Ryan a half hug..."

"See you next week..." Ryan said...

"Bye Cyn..." Daddy sighed...

"Bye Ryan..." Mommy sighed...

"Oh stop acting like you're not gonna see each other tomorrow!" Joshy said as everyone laughed...

When they got home, Mommy went upstairs without saying anything...

"She really mad at us?" Robert laughed...

"I don't think so..."

"Come here..." Robert breathed as he pulled Bri into a kiss...

"Mmm... what did I do to deserve that?"

"I still owe you from this morning..." he whispered in her ear as he moved his hands up and down her back...

"Oh Robert..." she moaned...

"I hope she wants to go live with them after they get married..." he breathed as he started kissing her on her neck...

"Me... too..." she panted...

"Go check on Cyn... I'll see you later..."

"I love you..."

"I love you too..." he breathed as he kissed her again and then he went into the library, sat in his chair, and turned on the television...

"Cyn?"

"Yes Mommy?"

"Can I come in?"

"Sure..." Bri opened the door, went inside, closed the door, and went to sit on the bed...

"We need to talk..."

"Okay..." Mommy sighed as she sat up and leaned back against the headboard...

"Are you mad at us?"

"No Mommy..." Mommy laughed...

"Good – 'cause I need to talk to you..."

"Are you mad because I didn't tell you I was pregnant?"

"No..."

"Well what's wrong then?"

"I need to take you to the doctor..."

"You do? Why?"

"You said you think your baby is due in December – that means you haven't had your period since March..."

"Yes..."

"The first trimester of your pregnancy is the most important..."

"Mommy?"

"Yes Cyn?"

"Do you think something's wrong with my baby?"

"No... but..."

"Mommy... what's wrong?"

"Do you remember when you had appendicitis?"

"Yea..."

"You had to have surgery..."

"I remember..."

"Well... the doctor said there was a chance you could develop scar tissue from the surgery..."

"Okay – but what does this have to do with my baby?"

"We need to make sure you don't have any scar tissue near your fallopian tubes or your uterus..."

"Do you think that's what happened Mommy?"

"No... I just want to be sure – besides – you need to see a doctor anyway..."

"What's she gonna do?"

"A basic gyn exam, breast exam, pap smear, and ultra sound..."

"Okay Mommy – I'll go to the doctor..."

"Good – we'll go see LuAnn tomorrow..."

"Her name is LuAnn?"

"Yes..."

"Can Ryan come?"

"If you want him to..."

"I want him to..."

"Okay then..." Bri said as she got up...

"Don't worry Mommy – I'm fine..." Mommy said as she got up and hugged her mother...

"You know I love you – right?"

"Yes Mommy..."

"Good – I'm gonna go spend some time with your Dad..." she said as she left and closed the door...

"How'd it go?" Robert asked as Bri sat down..."

"I'm more worried than she is..." Bri sighed...

"Worried? Why?"

"You remember when she had appendicitis?"

"Yea..."

"After she healed we went for her check-up..."

"Yes we did – she's fine..."

"Robert..." Bri whispered as she started crying..."

"Baby... No..." Robert said as he got up from the chair, went over to the couch, and pulled her up into a hug...

"I'm sorry..."

"What's wrong?"

"The doctor told me she has scar tissue on her fallopian tubes..."

"Why didn't you tell me?"

"You were so scared... I didn't want you to worry..."

"You don't think she's pregnant – do you?"

"Nooo..." Bri cried...

"Stop that..." Robert said as kissed her...

"The doctor told me she might not be able to have children..."

"You didn't tell her that... did you?"

"No..."

"I'm glad you didn't..."

"Do you forgive me?"

"There's nothing to forgive..."

"What if she's not pregnant?"

"She's pregnant..."

"Oh so now you're sure?"

"Did you see how much food your daughter ate earlier?"

"She ate a lot..." Bri laughed...

"Yes she did..."

"I love you..."

"I love you too..."

"You ready to go upstairs?"

"Yea..."

"Hello?"

"Hi Ryan..."

"What's wrong?"

"Mommy's worried about me..."

"She told you that?"

"Not in those words... but yea..."

"What'd she say?"

"She said I need to go to the doctor right away..."

"Oh boy..."

"She said the first trimester is the most important..."

"The first trimester?"

"Ryan – I haven't had my period since March..."

"Cyn! Why didn't you tell me?"

"Please don't be mad..."

"I'm not mad Cyn – but you could be 3 month's pregnant..."

"We'll find out tomorrow..."

"Tomorrow?"

"My mother's taking me to the doctor tomorrow..."

"What time?"

"I don't know – but I want you to come..."

"I'll be there – just let me know when..."

"Tomorrow morning... as soon as you wake up..."

"Okay – I'll see you first thing in the morning..."

"Oh Robert..."

"Didn't I tell you I owed you from this morning?" he growled as he started swirling his tongue around her clit...

"Yes Robert... Yes!" Bri moaned...

"Oh my God!" Mommy groaned...

"What's wrong?" Daddy asked...

"My parents are having sex!"

"Sorry..." Daddy laughed...

"I'm going downstairs!" Mommy exclaimed as she jumped up off the bed, flung open her door, and flew down the stairs...

"They still at it?"

"I'm sure they are..." Mommy answered as she sat in her father's chair and turned on the television...

"I think we should live with your parents..." Daddy laughed...

"Oh my God – why?" Mommy laughed...

"So they can hear us have sex..." Daddy laughed...

"Eww! No!" Mommy laughed...

"We can jump on the bed and pretend like we're having sex – and make noise..." Daddy laughed...

"Now that's funny!" Mommy laughed...

"How long are you gonna be downstairs?"

"At least an hour – The Chi's on..."

"Oh shit – thanks for reminding me – I'll see you tomorrow – I love you..."

"I love you too..." Mommy said and then Daddy hung up...

"If we ever do that to you – I'm sorry..." Mommy said as she rubbed her stomach...

"It's okay Mommy..." I said as I started releasing endorphins and serotonin...

"Good morning Beautiful..." Robert said as he kissed Bri awake...

"Mmmm... Good morning..."

"We scared the shit out of Cyn..." Robert laughed...

"You're the one that wanted to pay me back..." Bri laughed...

"You should 'a thought about that yesterday..." he laughed...

"I did..." she laughed...

"What time do you need to be at the doctor?"

"What time is it now?"

"It's a little after 8..."

"Let me get up..." she said as she tried to get out of bed and Robert pulled her back down...

"Robert..."

"Shhh..." he breathed as he pulled her into a kiss...

"Robert... I can't..."

"Fine..." he sighed...

"I'll make it up to you when we get home..."

"You promise?" Bri didn't answer him – she got up out the bed, slipped out of her lingerie, and stood there naked in front of him...

"See... you keep playing with me..." he said as he jumped up outta bed and grabbed her...

"Robert!" she squealed...

"Umm... Mommy?"

"Yes Cyn?"

"What time are we leaving?"

"I'm going to call the doctor now..."

"Okay – are we having breakfast?"

"Are you hungry?"

"Yea..."

"Okay – we can have breakfast..."

"I'm already dressed – I'll go make something..."

"Okay – thanks..."

"I'm making coffee too..."

"Thank you Cyn..."

"You're welcome..." Mommy said as she hurried downstairs and her father bust out laughing...

"Oh shut up..." Bri laughed...

"You better hurry up and get in that bathroom..."

"You better hurry up and join me..."

"Oh – okay!" he said as he jumped followed her into the bathroom and she started the shower...

"Good morning..."
"Hi Ryan..." Cyn laughed...
"What's so funny?"
"My parents!" she laughed...
"Oh my God! They're still at it?" Daddy laughed...
"Yes!" Mommy laughed...
"I wonder if my parents go at it like that..."
"I bet they do..." Mommy laughed...
"I hope we go at it like that when we get to be their age..."
"Oh so you want us to embarrass our kids?"
"Did you say kids?"
"Yea..."
"So you want more than one?"
"Yea..."
"I love you..."
"I love you too..."
"I'm making breakfast..."
"I'm on my way..." Daddy said and then he hung up...

"Good morning – thank you for calling Dr. Russo's office – how may I help you?"
"Hi Shelly – It's Mrs. Lawrence..."
"Hi Bri – how are you?"

"I need an appointment today if you have one..."

"Is everything okay?"

"I hope so..."

"Oh boy – let me see... we had a cancellation for 10:30 – can you make it then?"

"We sure can..."

"We? Is your husband coming with you?"

"No – my daughter and her fiancée..."

"Her fiancée? She's engaged?"

"He asked her to marry him yesterday..."

"Oh wow – congratulations!"

"Thank you..."

"I'll see you at 10:30..." Shelly said and then she hung up...

"What time is the appointment?" Robert asked...

"10:30..." Bri sighed...

"She'll be fine..." he said as he pulled her into a hug and held her..."

"I hope so..." she sighed...

"I need you to act as if everything is okay..."

"I know..."

"You don't want Cyn to pick up on how you're feeling..."

"Ryan's coming with us..."

"That's good – he'll keep her occupied..."

"Let's go – I smell coffee..." she said as Robert opened the door and they went downstairs to the kitchen...

"Good morning Daddy..." Cyn said...

"Good morning – thanks for making coffee..."

"You're welcome – I made some breakfast sandwiches..."

"Oh yea – what kind?"

"Bacon, egg, and cheese – but I made one without cheese for you Daddy..."

"Thank you Cyn..." Robert said as Daddy knocked on the door...

"Coming!" Mommy exclaimed as she hurried to answer the door...

"Good morning – coffee smells good..." Daddy said...

"You want some?"

"Sure..."

"C'mon..." Mommy said as she pulled Daddy into the dining room...

"Good morning Ryan..." Bri said...

"Good morning Mrs. Lawrence – I mean Mom..."

"Good morning Ryan..." Robert said...

"Good morning Dad..."

"I'll get the sandwiches..." Cyn said as she hurried into the kitchen...

"Le'me go help this child..." Bri laughed...

"Are you ready for today?" Robert asked...

"Yea..."

"You better be..." Robert laughed as Mommy and Bri came back in the dining room with the plates...

"Here Daddy – this is yours..." Mommy said...

"Thank you Cyn...

"You're welcome – I'll go get coffee..."

"I'll be right back..." Bri laughed as she followed Cyn into the kitchen....

"I can't believe she's in her first trimester already..." Daddy said...

"What did you just say?" Robert asked...

"Oooppsss..."

"Here's coffee..." Cyn said as she put a cup of coffee in front of Ryan and sat down...

"Here Robert..." Bri said as she gave him a cup of coffee...

"Thank you Dear..."

"You're welcome..." Bri said as she sat down and they started eating...

"What time is our appointment Mommy?"

"10:30..."

"Oh..."

"Bri! How are you?" the receptionist asked as they walked in…

"I'm good…" Bri answered…

"I see you brought a friend…"

"Yes I did – this is my daughter Cyn – and this is her fiancé Ryan…" she said as she introduced her…

"Nice to meet you Cyn – congratulations on your engagement..."

"Thank you – and this is my fiancé Ryan..."

"Nice meeting you Ryan – I'm Shelly..."

"Nice to meet you Shelly..." Ryan said...

"Your mother said you need to see the doctor..." Shelly said...

"Yes I do..." Cyn beamed...

"Is this your first time here?"

"Yes it is..."

"Okay – I need you to give me your insurance card and fill out these forms..." she said as she gave Cyn a clipboard with 10 sheets full of questions...

"Oh my God – I have to fill out all these?" Cyn laughed...

"I'm afraid so..." Shelly answered...

"Here's her insurance card..." Bri said as she pulled the card out her wallet and handed it to Shelly...

"Oh my God – Ryan!" Cyn laughed as she pointed to the questions...

"What the hell?" Ryan exclaimed...

"I know – right?" she laughed...

"That's funny – we usually get an angry reaction..." Shelly said...

"Oh boy – the questions..." Bri laughed...

"Yes!" Cyn and Ryan exclaimed in unison...

"Do people actually answer these?" Cyn asked...

"Sometimes..." Shelly answered...

"They're so personal!" Cyn exclaimed...

"You don't have to answer anything you don't want to..." Shelly said...

"I'm not – don't worry!" Cyn laughed...

"Hello Bri..." Dr. Russo said as she came out into the waiting area...

"Hi LuAnn..." Bri said...

"Are you here to see me today?"

"No – my daughter Cyn is here to see you – and this is her fiancé Ryan..."

"Hello – I'm Dr. LuAnn Russo – but you can call me LuAnn..."

"Hi LuAnn – I'm Cyn – and this is my fiancé Ryan..."

"Nice to meet you Cyn, nice to meet you Ryan – Cyn, please come with me..."

"Can Ryan come?"

"If that'd make you more comfortable – sure..." she answered as Cyn and Ryan got up and they both followed LuAnn into the examination room...

"Ryan – you sit here – Cyn – I need you to take everything off, put this gown on with the opening to the front, and sit on the table – I'll be right back..." LuAnn said and then she went to leave the room...

"Where are you going?" Cyn asked...

"I'm giving you privacy..."

"Aren't you going to see me naked anyway?"

"Yes..."

"Well you might as well stay..." Cyn laughed...

"I need to go get your papers – get undressed – I'll be right back..." she said as she left the room...

"Here Ryan – hold my clothes..."

"Okay..." he said as LuAnn knocked on the door...

"Come in..." Cyn said...

"Cyn – we need to talk..."

"Okay..."

"You didn't answer a lot of the questions..."

"I don't think you need to know all my business!" Cyn laughed...

"Cyn – I don't care how many partners you've had – I don't care about oral sex – I don't care about anal sex – you're right – that's not my business – but I am concerned about the other questions..."

"What other questions?"

"Why haven't you had a pap smear?"

"I just never had one..."

"Cyn – annual pap smears are important – especially among young black women – it's your best chance at preventing cervical cancer and HPV..."

"I know..."

"Why did you come here today?"

"Because I'm pregnant..."

"You're pregnant? How do you know you're pregnant?"

"I took a pregnancy test at home..."

"Congratulations..."

"Thank you..." Cyn said...

"Okay – we're going to do a couple of things – first – I need to take some blood..."

"Why?"

"We need to know your blood type – if you're positive – it's not an issue – if you're negative – we need to monitor you closely – and you'll need a shot to protect you and your baby if you want more children..."

"I don't understand..."

"Okay – your immune system contains protective substance called antibodies that fight off bacteria or any material that your immune system doesn't recognize...

"Okay..."

"Antibodies also attack antigens that aren't present in your natural blood type – so if your blood is positive – you're okay – if your blood type is RH Negative and your baby is positive – your immune system will make antibodies against your baby's red blood cells...

"Oh wow..."

"If that happens then your baby could be born with jaundice – that's a yellowing of the skin and whites of the eyes, lethargy, or low muscle tone..."

"Can you protect my baby?"

"Yes – that's why I'm taking your blood. It takes time – that doesn't happen overnight and it doesn't happen often – but it does happen…"

"It is possible I could have a miscarriage?"

"Let's not worry about that right now..."

"Okay…"

"Okay – I'm going to take some blood – we'll send it over and find out what your blood type is – and we'll take it from there – okay?"

"Okay…"

"Ryan – do you know what your blood type is?"

"I'm O Positive…"

"Okay – I'll note that in Cyn's chart…" she said as she prepared the needle and tubes… "Are you ready Cyn?"

"I'm ready…"

"Okay – hold still – it'll just be a pinch…" she said as she inserted the needle and took Cyn's blood… "Okay – we'll get this out to the lab – now I need to do a breast exam – lie down on your back…"

"Okay…"

"Have you ever done a self-breast exam?"

"No…"

"Well – when you come for your annual checkup, the breast exam is part of that…"

"Okay…"

"Any tenderness?" she asked as she examined Cyn's breasts…

"A little..."

"Everything seems fine – now – I need you to scoot down to the bottom of the table and open your legs...

"Okay..."

"Since you've never had a pap smear – I'm going to give you one..."

"But I'm already pregnant..."

"Yes I know – but we're going to use this first one to compare to each one you get afterwards..."

"Okay..."

"If you feel any discomfort – let me know..."

"Okay..."

"I'm going to insert the speculum into your vagina – it's going to hold your vagina open so I can see your cervix – then I'll do your pap smear – then we'll take it out..."

"Does it hurt?"

"No..."

"Can I see it?"

"Sure..." she answered as she held up the plastic speculum...

"That doesn't look so bad..."

"It's not – it might be a little uncomfortable though..."

"Okay..."

"Are you ready?"

"I'm ready..."

"Okay – here goes – try to relax..."

"Okay..."

"Alright – it's in – I'm going to open it now – you okay?"

"I'm okay..."

"Hmmm... Ryan – come take a look..."

"Okay..." Ryan said as he got up and went to look between Cyn's legs...

"That's the cervix..."

"Oh... okay..."

"I'm going to take this swab, get a sample, and then we'll send it to the lab..."

"Okay..." Ryan said...

"How you doing Cyn?"

"I'm okay..."

"Okay – I'm swabbing the cervix now – you okay?"

"I'm okay..."

"Okay – I'm done – I'm going to take the speculum out now..."

"Okay..."

"Now I'm going to check your ovaries and your fallopian tubes – I'm going to put on a glove, put some jelly on the glove, and stick my fingers in your vagina..."

"Why?"

"I need to check the position of your cervix and I can only do that with my hand..."

"Okay..."

"Here I go – you okay?"

"I'm okay..."

"Any tenderness when I push here?"

"A little..."

"How 'bout here?"

"Owww!"

"I'm sorry – are you okay?"

"I'm okay..."

"Okay – now for the best part..."

"The best part?"

"Yes – I'm going to do a sonogram and see how pregnant you are..." she answered as she squirted jelly on Cyn's stomach...

"That's cold!"

"Sorry about that..." she said as she smoothed it on Cyn's stomach and turned on the machine... "Oh my goodness..."

"Is something wrong?" Ryan asked...

"Cyn – when was your last period?"

"March..."

"Hmmm..." LuAnn said as she kept looking at the screen...

"Is everything okay?" Cyn asked...

"I'll be right back..." LuAnn said as she got up and left the room...

"Ryan... I'm scared..."

"Don't be scared Cyn..." Ryan said as he took her hand..."

"Hi Cyn – I'm Dr. Kay... she said as she came into the examination room...

"Is everything okay?"

"LuAnn asked me to come in and take a look at what's happening..." she answered...

"Umm... what's happening?" Ryan asked...

"Oh my God – I don't believe it..." Dr. Kay whispered...

"I didn't believe it either..." LuAnn said...

"Is there something wrong with my baby?" Cyn asked with tears in her eyes...

"Your baby's perfect..." LuAnn answered...

"Can I see?" Cyn asked...

"Kay – could you go ask Mrs. Lawrence to come in?" LuAnn asked...

"Sure..." Dr. Kay said as she went to go get Bri...

"Cyn – look – I can see our baby – turn your head!" Ryan exclaimed as Dr. Kay came back in the room with Bri...

"What's wrong LuAnn?" Bri asked...

"Our baby's perfect Mommy..." Cyn cried...

"It's a miracle you're even pregnant..." LuAnn said..."

"It's a miracle I'm pregnant? I don't understand..." Cyn said...

"Look at the screen..." LuAnn said...

"I see my baby..." Cyn beamed...

"Do you see this?" LuAnn said as she went over the area where she pushed on Mommy and it hurt..."

"Yea..."

"That's scar tissue..."

"It is?"

"Your fallopian tube is completely blocked..."

"Oh my God – how did I get pregnant then?"

"See this over here?" LuAnn asked...

"I see it..." Cyn answered...

"That's your other fallopian tube – there's no scar tissue over there..."

"Ooohhh..."

"I have patients that come see me with blocked fallopian tubes... and they cry when I tell them they probably won't be able to have children... and here you are..."

"Hi My Christmas Miracle..." Cyn cried...

"Hi Mommy!" I beamed...

"Hi My Christmas Miracle – I'm your Grandma..."

"Hi My Grandma!" I beamed...

"I'm gonna take a few pictures..." LuAnn said as she took pictures...

"How many months am I?" Cyn asked...

"I'd say you're about 12 weeks..." LuAnn answered...

"We're having a baby..." Ryan whispered as he took Cyn's hand and started to cry…

"I love you Ryan…"

"I love you too…" Daddy said as he leaned over to kiss Mommy…

"I'll print these pictures for you…" LuAnn said as she printed the sonogram for them and let them have their moment… "Here you go…" she said as she handed them to Ryan…

"Thank you LuAnn…" he sniffed as he put the pictures in his pocket…

"Okay Cyn – you can sit up now – but I have a couple of questions I need to ask…"

"Okay…"

"How's your appetite?"

"I'm always hungry!" Mommy laughed...

"I'm starting you on prenatal vitamins – I need you to take them every day – understand?"

"Yes Maam..."

"Okay – any fatigue?"

"Sometimes..."

"Bri - keep an eye on her – and make sure she gets plenty of rest..."

"Yes Maam..." Bri acknowledged...

"Any fainting?"

"No..."

"Okay – I need to see you again in two weeks..."

"Okay..."

"You're about three months – about 12 weeks – you should have your baby a couple of days before Christmas - okay - here's what you need to do..."

"Yes LuAnn?"

"You need to eat, you need to take your prenatal vitamins, you need to rest, and you need to see me in two weeks – got it?"

"Got it..."

"Okay – you can get dressed – here's the prescription for the prenatal vitamins – I'll see you in two weeks – congratulations again..." she said as she left the room...

"I'll see you outside..." Bri said as she got up and left the room...

"Ryan..." Cyn whispered as she started to cry and Daddy grabbed her into a hug...

"I know…" he whispered as he moved her hair out of her face and cried with her…

"I'm so happy…"

"Me too…" Mommy got dressed and then they both went out to the reception desk...

"Shelly?"

"Yes Cyn?"

"I need to make another appointment for two weeks from today…"

"Okay – how's 9 a.m.?"

"That's fine…" Cyn sighed…

"When we got home, Bri couldn't wait to see Robert...

"How'd everything go?"

"Oh Robert..." Bri whispered as she started crying...

"Baby – what's wrong?"

"Hi Daddy..." Mommy said as she walked in with Daddy...

"Everything alright?"

"Everything's fine..." Daddy said as he took the pictures of me out his pocket...

"Is this my grandchild?' Robert asked as he started tearing up...

"The doctor said she's perfect..." Mommy said...

"She?"

"I think so..."

"The doctor said it's a miracle I got pregnant..." Mommy said...

"I told your mother everything would be fine..."

"I knew you were worried about me!" Mommy exclaimed...

"How are you feeling?" Robert said as he pulled Mommy to him and started rubbing her stomach...

"I'm feeling good Daddy..."

"Hi My Christmas Miracle... I'm your Grandpa..."

"Hi Grandpa..." I beamed...

"Ryan – we need a copy of this sonogram..." Robert said as he gave the pictures back to Daddy...

"I'll need a few copies – otherwise my parent's won't give it back..." Daddy laughed as he put the pictures in his pocket...

"C'mon Ryan..." Mommy said as she took Daddy's hand and pulled him...

"Where are we going?" Daddy laughed...

"Upstairs!" Mommy exclaimed as she pulled Daddy out the library and they went upstairs...

"I told you so..." Robert said as he pulled Bri into a hug...

"Yes you did..." Bri sighed...

"So what else did the doctor say?"

"She said it's a miracle Cyn's pregnant..."

"Really?"

"Robert – one of her fallopian tubes is completely blocked..."

"Oh wow..."

"I'm so happy..."

"So am I..."

"Now if we can just convince those two to move in with his parents..." Bri laughed...

"I love you so much..." Daddy breathed as he kissed Mommy...

"I love you too..." Daddy moved Mommy backwards towards the bed and pushed her down...

"Ryan – we can't..."

"Ssshhh..." Daddy said as he got on the bed beside Mommy and started kissing her... "Your room's smaller than mine..."

"Mmm hmmm..."

"I'm not sure where my stuff would fit..."

"Mmm hmmm..."

"Cyn..."

"Yes Ryan..." Mommy breathed...

"We need to talk..."

"Okay..." Mommy sighed...

"I've been looking on realtor.com..."

"You have?"

"Yea – c'mon – I'll show you..." Daddy said as he got up off the bed and went to turn on Mommy's computer...

"Okay..." Mommy sighed as she got up and went to sit with Daddy...

"Harvard is in Cambridge..."

"Uh huh..."

"Their business school is in Boston..."

"Uh huh..."

"We'd have to move to Cambridge or Boston to be close to campus..."

"We don't have the money to do that..."

"Exactly – look how expensive some of these properties are..." Daddy said as he showed Mommy condos in Cambridge and Boston...

"Oh my God!" I didn't know they were so expensive!"

"Neither did I – so I decided to look at some condos in cities near Harvard and I found some that are more affordable..." Daddy said as he showed her condos in Dorchester, West Roxbury, Mattapan, and Milford in Massachusetts...

"These are nice..." Mommy said...

"Yes – they're nice – and they're more affordable – but they're all a little over 20 minutes away – and Milford is about 40 minutes away..."

"Oh wow..."

"I don't think we should move to Massachusetts..."

"I don't either..." Mommy sighed...

"But I don't think we should live with our parents either..."

"Well what should we do then?"

"We'll get married after graduation..."

"Okay..."

"After we get married, we'll live with our parents..."

"But I thought you said..."

"Cyn – let me finish..."

"Okay..."

"I think we should live with our parents until we can move out..."

"I thought we were going to college?"

"We are..."

"We're not going right away?"

"We might not go to college until January..."

"Why can't we start school in September?"

"We can – but if we start looking for our own place now, we could be in our own place before the baby's born..."

"What if we can't afford a two-bedroom?"

"We can't right now..."

"So we're gonna get a one-bedroom?"

"Yes..."

"So the baby will sleep in the room with us?"

"Yes – and we'll be close to our parents..."

"We will?"

"Condos are more affordable here..."

"How will we get to school from here? Harvard is over 2 hours away..."

"I looked into that too..."

"You did?"

"Yea – we can take classes online, but we need to take four classes on campus to get our degrees..."

"How can we do that if we stay here?"

"We can take eight credits in the summer, or we can take four credits in the first three-week session and 4 credits in the second three-week session...

"What about weekends?"

"We can do that too – you earn four credits in two weekends..."

"This sounds good – but what are we gonna do for childcare? Childcare is expensive..."

"I'm going to work, and you're going to stay home with the baby..."

"You don't have a job yet..."

"That's only temporary..."

"How can we afford our own place right away?"

"My grandmother left me some money..."

"Aww..."

"We won't be rich – but we'll have enough for a down-payment on something – and my parents already gave me a car, so we'll be fine..."

"I love you..."

"I love you too..."

"Now we just have to decide where we wanna live..." Mommy sighed...

"I still wanna live here..." Daddy laughed...

"You just wanna stick it to my parents..." Mommy laughed...

"C'mon – let's go show my parents our Christmas Miracle..." Daddy said as he got up...

"Okay!" Mommy squealed...

"Sure is quiet up there..." Bri said...

"What do you think they're doing?" Robert laughed...

"I wish we had a room downstairs..."

"I'm not giving up my library..." Robert breathed as he pulled Bri into a kiss...

"Bye Mommy! Bye Daddy!" Mommy yelled...

"Cyn – wait a minute..." Bri said as she came out the library...

"Yes Mommy?"

"Where are you going?"

"I'm going with Ryan – we'll be back later!" Mommy exclaimed as Mommy and Daddy hurried out the door...

"Ryan... don't stop..."

"I won't baby... Uuuggghhh..."

"Ryan... I'm cumming... I'm cumming..."

"Cum for me baby..."

"Aaaggghhh... Aaaggghhh... Aaaggghhh... Aaaggghhh..."

"Oh my God..." Daddy laughed...

“Now I know what you mean...” Mommy laughed...

“C’mon – let’s go in the kitchen – we still have some cake and pie left...” Daddy laughed as he took Mommy by the hand and led her into the kitchen...

“Uuuggghhh... Uuuggghhh... Uuuggghhh... Uuuggghhh...”

“Ryan...”

“Oh Joshy...”

“Ryan... stop...”

“Did you just tell me to stop?”

“There’s somebody in the house...”

“Let me go check it out...” Ryan said as he got up and put his clothes on...”

“I’m coming with you...” Joshy said as she started getting dressed. When they got to the top of the stairs, Ryan started laughing... “What’s so funny?”

“Honey – it’s Ryan...”

“Oh my God – I made you stop... I’m sorry...”

“That’s okay baby...”

“No it isn’t... but it will be...” Joshy said as she pulled Ryan towards the bedroom by his pants...

“Oh yea?”

“Yea...” Joshy answered as she pulled him back in the bedroom and closed the door...

"Which one would you like?" Daddy asked as he took the cake and pie out the refrigerator...

"Both..."

"Both it is..." Daddy said as he put a plate of cake and pie on the table with a fork...

"Thank you..."Mommy said as she started eating...

"Our Christmas Miracle sure has an appetite..." Daddy said as he sat down with a plate of cake...

"Ryan... Ryan... Ryan..."

"I'm cummin baby... I'm cummin..."

"I'm cumming with you..."

"Uuuggghhh! Uuuggghhh! Uuuggghhh!

"Aaaggghhh! Aaaggghhh! Aaaggghhh!"

"Damn Baby..." Ryan breathed...

"I'm gonna make you stop more often..." Joshy panted...

"It was good... wasn't it?"

"Hell yea..."

"If these kids move in here... we're gonna have a problem..."

"The hell you say – you gonna fuck me regardless..."

"Yes Baby..." Ryan breathed as he kissed her hard... "Yeesss..."

"It's quiet..." Mommy said...

"For now..." Daddy laughed...

"You think they're goin' for another round?"

"You mean a third round?" Daddy laughed...

"Do you think we'll be like them?"

"I'm sure gonna try to be..." Daddy laughed...

"C'mon – let's go in my room until they come down..."

"Okay..."

"C'mon – let's go downstairs..." Ryan said...

"Don't you wanna stay here?" Joshy asked seductively...

"Baby... you know I wanna stay with you – but I wanna know what happened at the doctor..." Ryan said as he got up out the bed and started getting dressed...

"Okay – we'll go downstairs..."

"Ryan? Where are you?"

"I'm in here Dad..."

"Yes Dad..."

"Hey..."

"Hi Dad..."

"Hi Dad..." Mommy said...

"C'mon – let's go in the living room..." Ryan said...

"Okay Dad – we're coming..." Daddy said as he and Mommy got up and went into the living room..."

"Hi Ryan..." Joshy said as she pulled him into a hug...

"Hi Mom..."

"Hi Cyn..." she said as she pulled Cyn into a hug...

"Hi Mom..."

"Aww... you called me Mom..."

"So – she called me Dad!" Ryan laughed...

"He's a picture of our Christmas Miracle..." Daddy said as he pulled the sonogram out of his pocket and gave it to his mother...

"Oh my God! How many weeks are you?"

"I'm 12 weeks..." Mommy answered...

"So our grandchild well be here at Christmas?" Ryan asked as he took the sonogram and looked at the pictures...

"Yes Dad..." Daddy answered..."

"Is that why you called the baby your Christmas Miracle?" Ryan asked...

"I call her My Christmas Miracle because the doctor told me it's a miracle I'm pregnant..." Mommy answered...

"Oh my God – Cyn – are you okay?" Joshy asked...

"I have some scar tissue on one of my fallopian tubes so the doctors thought I couldn't have children..."

"The doctor told us our baby's perfect..." Daddy said...

"Hi My Christmas Miracle... I'm your Grandma..." Joshy said as she pulled up Mommy's shirt and kissed her stomach...

"That tickles!" Mommy and I both said in unison as we laughed...

"Hi My Christmas Miracle – I'm your Grandpa – I can't wait to meet you..." Ryan said as he pulled Cyn into a hug...

"Ummm... Dad?"

"Yes son..."

"I need those pictures..." Daddy laughed...

Mommy and Daddy had a busy week preparing for graduation. They tied for valedictorian so they prepared a speech to read together. When Mommy saw her friend Ally, she hurried to catch up to her...

"Ally... Wait up..."

"Hi Cyn..."

"I haven't seen you in a few days..."

"I know – I've been busy..."

"Ally – I know something's bothering you – talk to me..."

"You wanna know what's bothering me? You! That's what's bothering me!"

"Ally... what'd I do?"

"What haven't you done? You have the perfect boyfriend – you have perfect grades –

you're both perfect valedictorians – you both have perfect scholarships – you have the perfect life ahead of you – it isn't fair!" she cried...

"Ally..." Cyn sighed as she hugged Ally and let Ally cry on her shoulder...

"I'm pregnant..."

"Oh Ally..."

"Chip doesn't want anything to do with me – he told me to get an abortion..."

"Ally... I'm so sorry..." Cyn said as she teared up...

"I love him so much... and he doesn't want me..."

"I'm sorry..."

"I can't keep my baby – if my parents find out I'm pregnant – they'll put me out..."

"No they won't – they love you..."

"Yes they will Cyn! My father already told me I better not come home pregnant!"

"I don't think they'll put you out Ally..."

"I went to talk to Chip's parents – they wrote me a check to pay for an abortion!" Ally cried...

"Oh my God..."

"His father said his son has his whole life ahead of him and he doesn't need to be tied down with a baby!"

"I'm so sorry Ally..."

"What am I gonna do?"

"Nothing..."

"Nothing?"

"Have you been to a doctor?"

"No..."

"You need to go to a doctor..."

"I can't go to Planned Parenthood – it'll be all over school!"

"Do you still have that check Chip's parents gave you?"

"Yes..."

"How much is it for?"

"$1,500..."

"Good – I'll take you to my doctor..."

"Cyn – my parents can't find out I'm pregnant..."

"You're 18 – they won't tell your parents..."

"How am I gonna pay for a doctor with no insurance?"

"You're not gonna pay for anything – Chip's parents wrote you a check – let them pay for it..."

"Will you go with me?"

"Of course..."

"Please don't tell anybody..."

"I won't Ally..."

"Wait a minute..."

"What's wrong?"

"Why did you have a doctor – oh my God – you went to get birth control – are you and Ryan having sex?"

"Yea..."

"How was it? Tell me everything!"

"I'm not telling you everything..." Cyn laughed...

"Cyn!"

"Ryan made love to me..." Mommy sighed...

"Aww..."

"It was everything I thought it would be..."

"I wish I could say that..." Ally sighed...

"What happened?"

"I don't wanna talk about it..."

"Was it that bad?"

"Promise you won't tell anybody..."

"I won't tell anybody Ally – I promise..."

"I think Chip was a virgin..."

"Ooohhh..."

"It was like he didn't know what he was doing..."

"Maybe he was just nervous..."

"It was more than that – he couldn't find the hole..."

"Oh my God!" Mommy laughed...

"Cyn!"

"I'm sorry – I'm not laughing at you – I'm laughing at him..."

"After he found the hole, he basically just humped me until he came..."

"I'm sorry Ally..."

"At least I was right about one thing..."

"What's that?"

"It didn't hurt..."

"That's a good thing..."

"I was really nervous about that..."

"I was too..."

"So it was everything you dreamed it would be huh?"

"Yea..." Mommy sighed...

"Did he... Never mind..."

"Did he come?"

"I know he did that..."

"What are you asking me Ally?"

"Did you?"

"Did I come?"

"Yea..."

"Yes..."

"I didn't..."

"Did you like it?"

"What do you mean?"

"Did you like having sex?"

"Yea..."

"Me too..."

"I was hoping there'd be a next time..." Ally sighed...

"There will be..."

"Can I ask you something?"

"Sure..."

"Did you do it again?"

"You mean right after?"

"Yea..."

"No – we did it again the next day..."

"Ooohhh – you spent the night with him?"

"Yea..."

"I didn't..."

"Did you do it again?"

"Chip wanted to – but I told him I had to go..." Ally sighed...

"I have a confession – but you better not tell anybody!"

"Cyn! Why would you say that?"

"You're right – I'm sorry..."

"Tell me..."

"We didn't use protection either..."

"Oh my God! But you have a doctor so if you're not using protection... Oh my God! Are you pregnant?"

"Yes Ally..."

"Does Ryan know?"

"Yes..."

"Are you keeping it?"

"Yes..."

"And Ryan's okay with that?"

"Ryan's happy about the baby..."

"I wish Chip could be more like Ryan..." Ally sighed...

"I wish he could be too..."

"Where did I go wrong Cyn?" she cried...

"Ally no – don't cry – it's not you – it's him..."

"I'm going to have an abortion..."

"You are?"

"Yea..."

"You don't have to have an abortion – you can keep your baby if you want to..."

"I'm not going to be a single parent..."

"I'm so sorry you're going through this – I'll call my doctor and get an appointment for you right away..."

"Thank you Cyn – I couldn't get through this without you..."

"You won't have to..."

"Hey Ryan..." Chip said...

"Hey..."

"You ready for tonight's game?"

"I sure am..."

"You get any pussy yet?"

"That's none of your business..."

"When are you gonna give it up?"

"What the hell are you talking about?"

"Why are you waiting around for Cyn – you could have any girl you want!"

"I'm not like you..."

"Damn right you're not like me – I listened to my father..."

"What's that supposed to mean?"

"I broke up with Ally as soon as she gave me some pussy..." Chip laughed...

"That's fucked up!"

"What's fucked up about it – it's not like I raped her..."

"She loves you!"

"That's her problem..."

"What the fuck is wrong with you?"

"Oh my God – you're in love!"

"Yes I am..."

"See – that's the difference between you and me – my father told me don't try to fall in love too soon – I have time for that later..."

"Oh so your father told you to fuck Ally and dump her?"

"Oh my God – do you hear yourself? You've got to be one of the dumbest guys I know – you could've had pussy a long time ago – but no – you wanna wait for the girl you looovvveee..." Chip laughed...

"See – that's the difference between you and me..." Daddy didn't realize the rest of his teammates had walked into the locker room...

"Since you looovvveee Cyn so much – why don't you ask her to marry you – at least you'll get some pussy on your wedding night!" Chip said as he bust out laughing along with his teammates...

"Damn man – you ain't hit that yet?"

"Oh shit – you jerkin' every night huh?"

"I ain't wait for shit – if the girl I'm wit' don't put out – I find one that will!"

"You better than me – if she didn't wanna give me no pussy – I would 'a took it!"

"Exactly!" Chip exclaimed as they all laughed at Daddy...

"Hey..." Ryan said as Daddy came in. Daddy didn't speak – he just went in his room and slammed the door...

"Is that Ryan slamming that door?" Joshy asked...

"Yea..." Ryan answered...

"What the hell's wrong with him?"

"I'm about to find out..." Ryan said as he knocked on the door...

"Come in..." Daddy sighed...

"You wanna talk about it?"

"I'm quitting the team..."

"Bad game?"

"Yea..."

"You've had bad games before – you've never come up in this house slamming doors..."

"I'm sorry Dad..."

"Ryan – what happened?"

"I lost the game..."

"You lost the game?"

"They got in my head..."

"Who?"

"All of them – mainly Chip..."

"What happened between you and Chip?"

"You can't tell Mom..."

"Your mother and I don't keep secrets..."

"Dad – remember when you said you couldn't talk to your father because you were embarrassed?"

"Yes... I remember..."

"Well... I wanna talk to you... but it's embarrassing... so please don't tell Mom – okay?"

"Okay..."

"Chip asked me if I was ready for the game – and I was... but then – outta nowhere – he asks me if I got any pussy yet..."

"I went through that..."

"You did?"

"The guys rode me every chance they got..."

"How'd you handle it?"

"I was messed up at first – but then I realized I was the luckiest man in the world..."

"That's how I feel about Cyn..."

"If that's how you really feel about her – what they say shouldn't matter..."

"It's not that simple..."

"Oh? That's not what you were thinking when you stood up to Robert..."

"He told you?"

"Hell yea he told me – and I was proud of you..."

"Thanks Dad..."

"Now if you can stand up to Robert – you can stand up to your teammates..."

"Dad – you weren't there..."

"Ryan – we've all been there..."

"I bet Chip's never been there..."

"I'll let you in on a secret..."

"Okay..."

"The guy that runs his mouth the most, gets the least..."

"Really?"

"Are you running your mouth?"

"No!"

"Exactly – now think about the guys on your team – who runs their mouth more than anybody else on the team?"

"Chip..." Daddy sighed...

"I'll leave you with this quote from Tony Brown..."

"Okay..."

"Sugar, Water, Sugar, Water, Sugar, Water – Next..."

"What does that mean?" Daddy laughed...

"Some will, some won't, so what – next..."

"How does that apply to the team?"

"Some will always run their mouth, some won't run their mouth at all, so what – I'm happy regardless – next..."

"Thanks Dad..."

"You're welcome..."

"Thank you for calling Dr. Russo's office – this is Shelly – how can I help you?"

"Hi Shelly – this is Cyn..."

"Hi Cyn – is everything okay?"

"I'm okay – I'm calling for my friend..."

"Your friend?"

"She wants to have an abortion..."

"Does your friend have insurance?"

"No..."

"Your friend should go to Planned Parenthood – it won't cost as much..."

"She can't go to Planned Parenthood – everybody we know goes there..."

"Well she'll need to pay up-front since she doesn't have insurance..."

"She can..."

"What's her name?"

"Ally Holloway..."

"Can she come in tomorrow at 4?"

"She'll be there..."

"Okay Cyn – we'll see you tomorrow..."

"Hi Cyn..."

"Hi Ally..."

"You have an appointment tomorrow at 4..."

"You're still going with me – right?"

"Yes Ally..."

"Thank you Cyn..."

"You're welcome – I'll see you tomorrow..."

"Hi Cyn..." Shelly said as Mommy walked in...

"Hi Shelly, this is my friend Ally..."

"Hi Ally – it's nice to meet you..."

"Hi..."

"Do you have insurance?"

"No..."

"You'll have to pay upfront since you don't have any insurance – we accept cash, credit cards, and personal checks – there's a fee of $30 if the check is returned...

"If the check is returned just send the bill to the name on the check..."

"Okay - here ya go – just fill these out – when you're done, bring them back to me – I'll make up a chart and Dr. Russo will take you in the back..."

"Thank you Shelly..." Ally said as she took the clipboard, looked at the forms, and started crying...

"You okay?" Mommy whispered as she touched Ally's shoulder...

"No..." she whispered as she shook her head...

"Here..." Mommy said as she offered Ally a pack of tissues...

"Thanks..."

"You'll be alright..." Mommy said as LuAnn called Ally's name and they went down the hall...

"Come here..." LuAnn said as she pulled Ally into a hug and Ally cried on her shoulder for a few minutes... "Have a seat..." Ally wiped her eyes and sat down next to Mommy... "My name's LuAnn..."

"Hi LuAnn..." Ally sniffed...

"I've looked over your chart..."

"Okay..."

"You stated that you're here for an abortion..."

"Yes... that's correct..." Ally answered as she started crying again...

"Are you sure about this?"

"Yes..."

"You don't seem like you're sure..."

"My boyfriend broke up with me... he doesn't want the baby..." she cried...

"Oh my God... I'm so sorry... Ally?"

"Yes?"

"I'm going to take a urine sample, some blood, I'm gonna do a pelvic exam, and an ultrasound – we'll take it from there – you don't have to do anything today – okay?"

"Okay..."

"There's a cup in the bathroom – give me some urine, write your name on the cup, and come back in here..."

"Okay..." Ally sniffed as she got up and went to the bathroom. After Ally was done, she wrote her name on the cup and brought it back into the examining room...

"Thanks..." LuAnn said as she took the urine from her... "Okay – I'm gonna take some blood now – have you eaten anything?"

"No..."

"Would you like some coffee?"

"Yes..."

"How do you like it?"

"Light and sweet..."

"Okay – I'll get some blood – and then I'll get you some coffee..."

"Okay..." Ally said as she watched her prepare the tubes and the needle...

"You okay?"

"Yes... I'm okay..."

"I always ask – some people don't like needles..." she said as she took Ally's blood... "Would you like some coffee Cyn?"

"Yes please..."

"I'll be right back with your coffees..." LuAnn said as she took the blood, took the urine, and left the room...

"Shelly – do we have any coffee left?"

"Yes LuAnn..."

"Good – I need 2 cups – light and sweet – asap!"

"Are they for Cyn and Ally?"

"Yes..."

"Is Ally okay?" Shelly asked as she made the coffee and gave it to LuAnn..."

"She's as well as can be expected..." LuAnn answered as she went back down the hall...

"Here ya go..." LuAnn said as she gave Mommy and Ally coffee..."

"Thank you..." they both said in unison as Ally started gulping it down...

"Careful – it's hot!"

"I don't care..." Ally breathed as she finished it...

"I guess you needed that..."

"I did..."

"Okay – I'm going to do a pelvic exam – I need you to get undressed from the waist down – I'll leave if you want..."

"No – that's okay..." Ally said as she got undressed and got back up on the table...

"Okay – scoot down a bit so we can see what's going on..." Ally scooted down and LuAnn proceeded with a quick pelvic exam – by the time she felt her fingers inside her LuAnn was finished…

"Wow – that was quick…"

"Everything feels okay – now let's see how everything looks…" she said as she squirted the gel on Ally's stomach, turned on the machine, and started doing the sonogram… "Hmmm…"

"Is everything okay?"

"It's hard to tell what's going on – I need to do a transvaginal ultrasound…"

"What's a transvaginal ultrasound?"

"I'm going to put this long tube in your vagina – it will help me see your uterus, fallopian tubes, ovaries, cervix, and your vagina…"

"Will it hurt?"

"No – it doesn't use radiation – you might feel a little discomfort as I'm putting the transducer in, but that's it…"

"Okay…"

"Are you ready?"

"Yes…"

"Take a deep breath… then relax…" LuAnn said as she put the transducer in Ally's vagina… "Look… see that tiny little peanut right there?"

"Yes… I see it…"

"That's your baby..."

"I know…" Ally whispered as she started crying again…

"Do you want a picture?"

"Yes…" she sniffed…

"Okay… I'll print one out for you…" LuAnn said as she printed the picture for Ally…

"Can I get up now?"

"Yes Ally – I'm finished…" LuAnn answered as Ally got up and started getting dressed…

"How far along am I LuAnn?"

"I'd say you're about 2 weeks…"

"Okay…" Ally sighed…

"Okay – we've done the urine, the blood, the pelvic exam, the ultrasound. And the transvaginal ultrasound – now we need to talk about the abortion…"

"Okay…" Ally said as her eyes started tearing up…

"There are two categories of abortion…"

"Okay…" Ally said as tears ran down her cheeks and Mommy started crying too...

"Don't cry Mommy..." I said as I got really sad...

"Medical is where we use medication that causes the uterus to expel the pregnancy. Surgical is where the clinician removes the pregnancy…" Ally and Mommy continued crying as she continued… "The Medical Abortion uses a pill – it's similar to a miscarriage – you cramp, there's heavy bleeding, it can take longer, and require more appointments…"

"Oh my God… I can't…" Ally whispered…

"The Surgical Abortion feels more invasive, has more pain management, and is available quicker with fewer appointments. If you decide you want to go through with an abortion, you'll receive information on both procedures that explains the side effects and consequences. Before you get the abortion, both procedures require an education session and counseling…"

"I don't need education or counseling…" Ally said…

"Ally…" it's mandatory…"

"I'm not doing it…"

"We'll give you all the information… in case you change your mind…"

"LuAnn – you've been very compassionate – I appreciate your kindness – but I've heard enough – I'm not having an abortion…"

"What about your boyfriend?"

"Fuck him!" Ally exclaimed as she got up to leave. Mommy pulled Ally into a hug and they hugged each other…

"Ally – are you sure?"

"I'm keeping my baby!" Ally exclaimed...

"Yeeaaa!" I squealed as if they could hear me...

"C'mon – let's go give Chip the news!" Mommy laughed as they both got up to leave...

"Hi Cyn!" Daddy squealed when he saw Mommy...

"Hi Ryan..." Mommy sighed as they hugged each other...

"Are you staying for the game?"

"Ally – you wanna stay for the game?"

"I'm not sure yet..."

"Hi Ally – sorry – I didn't see you..." Daddy said...

"Hi Ryan – that's okay..."

"Ally! What are you doing here?"

"I just came to let you know I'm keeping the baby..." Ally beamed...

"What?! Are you crazy?!"

"You're pregnant?" Ryan asked as the other teammates gather around...

"Yes – I'm pregnant – and I'm keeping it..." Ally answered...

"Oh shit..." one of the team members gasped...

"It's over between us! I don't wanna be with you!" Chip yelled

"I'm still keeping our baby!" Ally exclaimed...

"We'll see about that..." Chip snapped as he started towards Ally and Daddy got between them...

"Leave her alone Chip..." Daddy said...

"Ryan – this has nothing to do with you – move!"

"No – leave her alone..." Daddy said...

"I swear to God – if you don't move..."

"You'll do what?" another teammate said as he stood alongside Ryan and the other teammates stood up...

"Why can't you be more like Ryan – Cyn's pregnant – she's keeping her baby – and Ryan's not making her get an abortion!" Ally snapped...

"Oh shit..." one of the teammates said. Ally put her hand over her mouth. Daddy looked at Mommy, and Mommy just shook her head back and forth...

"You don't wanna get an abortion? I got something for you Bitch – watch!" Chip said as he stormed off...

"What's going on here?" the coach asked as he came storming over to Daddy...

"I'm pregnant..." Ally said...

"I swear to God – if you guys would learn to use protection or just keep your dick in your got damned pants this shit wouldn't happen – Chip – you get your ass back here right now or you're off the team!" Chip ignored the coach and kept walking...

“Fuckin’ Bitch!” Chip exclaimed as he came inside...

“What the hell happened?” Ronald asked...

“She won’t get an abortion!”

“What the fuck you mean she won’t get an abortion? We wrote her a check...”

“Dad – she’s keeping the baby...”

“When did she tell you this?”

“Right before the coach threw me off the team...”

“You got thrown off the team?”

“Coach came over to find out what was going on – she announced she was pregnant – goodie-two-shoes Ryan decides to defend her – why can’t I be more like Ryan – Cyn’s pregnant – Ryan’s not making her get an abortion – coach is right – I should 'a used protection or kept my dick in my pants!"

"I told you this was gonna happen..." Regina sighed as she came in...

"Regina – not now!" Ronald yelled...

"Not now? When then? When he knocks someone else up? When he catches an STD?"

"Regina – I swear to God..."

"Oh shut the hell up..." Regina said as she stormed off..."

"Your mother's gonna make me smack the shit outta her..." Ronald laughed...

"Smack me Bitch!" Regina snapped as she drew back her hand and slapped Ronald across the mouth so hard his lip was bleeding. Chip stood there in shock. Ronald's breathing got really heavy, his chest started going up and down... and his nostrils flared... "Well? Whatcha gonna do mutha fucka!" Regina snapped...

"Dad – no!" Chip yelled as he jumped up and grabbed his father's arm...

"Move son..."

"No Dad... this isn't Mom's fault – leave her alone..."

"Fine – you're on your own – but first thing tomorrow you better get your ass back on that team so you don't lose your scholarship!" Ronald snapped as he stormed off to the library and slammed the door...

"Cyn – I'm sorry – I didn't mean to..." Ally tried to explain...

"Don't worry about it – I'm going to start showing soon anyway..."

"Good looking Ryan..." one of his teammates said...

"Congratulations man..."

"That's what's up..."

"Okay Ryan... I see you..."

"I'm happy for you man..."

"Congratulations Cyn..."

"Thank you..." Mommy said...

"Thanks guys..." Daddy said...

"Congratulations Ally..." one of the teammates said...

"I like the way you stood your ground with Chip..."

"I know – he should be glad she wants to have a baby with him...

"Thanks guys..." Ally said...

"Let's win this game..." Daddy said...

"Cyn – I gotta go..."

"You're not staying?"

"I need to go talk to my parents..." Ally sighed as she left...

"Mom? Dad?"

"Yes Ally?" Phillip answered...

"I need to talk to you..."

"Okay – we're in the living room..." Phillip said...

"I'm coming..." Ally said. When Ally got in the living room she stood there for a few moments... and then she started to cry...

"Ally – come here..." Alice said as she moved over so Ally could sit between them. Ally sat down and her mother held her as she cried...

"What's wrong Ally?" her mother asked as Ally's father rolled his eyes...

"I'm pregnant..."

"Okay..." her mother sighed as she continued to hold her...

"What did I tell you?" Ally's father said as he stood up...

"Daddy – I'm sorry – I didn't mean..."

"Didn't I tell you don't come in here pregnant?"

"Yes Daddy..." Ally sniffed...

"Come here..." her father commanded. Ally got up and went over to her father... "This is why I told you don't come in here pregnant..." he said as he pulled her into a hug and held her...

"I'm sorry Daddy..." she cried...

"Have you thought about what you wanna do?"

"I was gonna have an abortion – but I changed my mind..."

"Thank God!" her mother exclaimed...

"Chip broke up with me – he doesn't want anything to do with me... and he doesn't want the baby..."

"Chip? Chip Stuart?"

"Yes Daddy..." Ally couldn't understand why her father started smiling...

"Phillip? Are you okay?" her mother asked...

"I'm good..." he answered...

"Do you wanna see the baby?" Ally asked...

"You have a sonogram?" her mother asked...

"Yea..." Ally said as she took the sonogram out her pocket and showed it to her mother...

"Oh my God – she's so tiny!" her mother exclaimed...

"How you know it's a she? What if it's a he?" her father asked as he took the sonogram and looked at it...

"Did you go to Planned Parenthood?" her mother asked...

"No..."

"Where did you go?"

"I went to my friend's doctor..."

"Your friend? What friend?"

"I don't want her to be mad at me..."

"Why would she be mad at you?"

"Because she didn't want me to tell anybody she was pregnant... and I already did..."

"Well... since you don't wanna tell me..."

"I'll tell you the doctor's name..."

"Okay..."

"Dr. LuAnn Russo..."

"Why didn't you go to Planned Parenthood?"

"I didn't want everybody in school to know – but they will now..." Ally sighed...

"Ally – come sit down..." her mother said...

"What's going on?" her mother asked as her father sat down next to her..."

"Cyn took me to her doctor..."

"Cyn? Your friend? She's pregnant?"

"Yea..."

"Her parent's know?"

"Yea..."

"When did you go to the doctor?"

"Today..."

"What did the doctor say?"

"She didn't really say anything – she did a sonogram, took some blood, took some urine, and told me the different types of abortion I could get..."

"I thought you said you weren't getting an abortion?"

"I'm not..."

"You said everybody in school will know you're pregnant..."

"I went to the game... I saw Chip... I told him I was keeping the baby..."

"Good!"

"Ally?"

"Yes Daddy?"

"How did you pay for the doctor today?"

"I went to talk to Chip's parents..."

"You what?!"

"Daddy... please don't be mad... I thought maybe if I talked to them they'd convince Chip to reconsider... but Chips father told me his son has his whole life ahead of him and he didn't need to be tied down with a baby..."

"What does this have to do with the doctor?"

"Chip's father wrote me a check and told me to go get an abortion..."

"What! Oh hell no!" her mother exclaimed as her father smiled... "Phillip – what the hell are you smiling for?"

"I'm glad you asked me that..." Phillip answered as he took Ally's hand... "We represent the Stuarts... Chip is an heir to their throne... and I know where all their money is..."

"So that's why they didn't want Ally to have the baby!" her mother exclaimed...

"Oh my God..." Ally whispered...

"Ally – what did you do with the check?"

"I gave it to the receptionist at the doctor's office..."

"Good..."

"Phillip... what are you doing to do?"

"I'm going to call Ronald tomorrow... and I'm going to congratulate him on his grandchild... and when he asks me how I know... I'll let him know Ally's our daughter..."

"Hi Cyn – how was your day?" Bri asked. Cyn didn't answer her mother – she just burst out crying... "C'mon – I'll make us some tea..." Bri said as she took Cyn by the hand and led her into the kitchen...

"Where's Daddy?" Mommy asked...

"He's in the library – do you need me to go get him?"

"No..."

"Okay..." Bri said as she put the kettle on. Mommy wiped her face and sat there quiet as they both waited for the kettle to start whistling. After the kettle started whistling, Bri got two cups out the cabinet, got two Lipton tea bags, added sugar, added water, stirred them both, and brought them to the table... "I went to the doctor today..." Mommy sighed...

"Uh huh..." Bri said as they sipped their tea...

"Ally's pregnant..."

"Ooohhh..."

"Chip doesn't want anything to do with her – he told her to have an abortion..."

"Uh huh..."

"She didn't wanna go to Planned Parenthood because we know everybody there – so I told her I would take her to my doctor..."

"Does she have insurance?"

"She didn't tell her parents so she had to pay upfront..."

"How was she able to do that?"

"Chip's father wrote her a check to get an abortion so I told her to use that..."

"Uh huh..."

"Mommy... thank you for having me..."

"You're welcome Baby..."

"It was so sad... we were both crying... I don't see how anyone can do that..."

"Sometimes people don't have a choice..."

"Ally changed her mind – she's keeping her baby..."

"Good for her..."

"We went to the game to tell Chip..."

"Oh boy..."

"Chip yelled at her and told her he didn't want anything to do with her..."

"Oh my God – that's terrible!"

"Ryan got in front of Ally and told Chip to leave her alone – next thing you know – the whole team stood up for Ally..."

"Wow! Can I tell your father? Please?"

"Yea..."

"Oh thank God – what happened next?"

"Ally told him she was still keeping the baby – and then she asked him why can't you be more like Ryan – Cyn is pregnant and Ryan's not making her get an abortion..."

"Oh my God!"

"I wanted to slap her Mommy!"

"I bet!"

"Oh shoot – that's her calling me now..."

"You wanna talk to her?"

"Yea..."

"Okay – I'll go talk to your father..."

"Hello?"

"Are you mad at me?" Ally asked...

"Yessss..." Mommy laughed...

"I'm sorry..."

"How'd it go with your parents?"

"They're not putting me out..."

"See! I told you..."

"Guess what I found out?"

"What?"

"My Dad represents Chip's Dad... Chips an heir... and my Dad knows where all their money is..."

"Oh shit! Now I'm really glad you're keeping the baby..."

"Guess what else?"

"What?"

"My Dad said he's going to call Chip's father tomorrow and congratulate him on his grandchild..." Ally laughed...

"Oh my God! I wish I could be there!"

"Me too..."

"Robert!" Bri exclaimed as she hurried into the library and closed the door...

"Babe – can it wait? I'm watching the game..."

"I got tea!"

"Hold on – le'me see if they're gonna run this again later... looks like they're gonna run it again – okay – what's up?"

"Cyn took Ally to the doctor today..."

"She pregnant?"

"Yes – and guess what?"

"What?"

"Her boyfriend's father wrote the girl a check and told her to go get an abortion!"

"Get the fuck outta here!"

"They went to the doctor and Ally changed her mind – so they went to see Chip at the game..."

"Chip? Chip Stuart?"

"I dunno – why?"

"Aaahhhh haaaa...."

"What's so funny?"

"The Stuart's have money – Chip is the sole heir..."

"Oh my God – and I thought I had tea!" Bri laughed...

"What happened at the game?"

"Ally told Chip she was keeping her baby – Chip started yelling at her – Ryan stood up and told Chip to leave her alone!"

"What?!"

"Cyn said after Ryan stood up, the entire team stood up for Ally!"

"Hot Damn!" Robert exclaimed as they both laughed...

"Coach... can we talk?" Chip asked...

"I'm done with you Chip..."

"Please?"

"Fine..."

"I was hoping you'd reconsider taking me off the team..."

"You're wasting your breath..."

"I can't get another chance?"

"Look – I can't have the distractions – it'll cost us the championship – I need your head in the game – and you're using the wrong head right now..."

"Tell me what I can do to fix it..."

"That's your father's job – not mine..."

"Excuse me?"

"I'm not the one that needs to tell you how to be a man..."

"If I fix it – will you let me back on the team?"

"We have a game tomorrow night – your ass better be there on time – and you better have your head on straight – or I'm done – you understand me?"

"Thanks coach – you won't regret this!" Chip yelled as he ran out his office...

"I better not..." he sighed as he shook his head...

"So when are you due?" Ally asked Mommy...

"I'm due at Christmas..."

"Aww... that's nice..."

"Yea – my parents are happy..."

"Ally – can we talk?" Chip asked as he walked up to Mommy and Ally...

"There's nothing left for us to talk about..." Ally answered without turning around...

"You're having my baby..."

"Oh so now you care about the baby? The baby you wanted me to get rid of?"

"Can we talk? Please?"

"I guess..." Ally sighed...

"You want me to wait for you?"

"She doesn't need you to wait for her!" Chip snapped...

"See – this is what I'm talking about – leave me the fuck alone..." Ally said as she started to walk away...

"Ally – I'm sorry – wait..."

"Don't apologize to me – apologize to her..."

"I'm sorry Cyn..."

"Mmm hmm..." Mommy said as she rolled her eyes...

"Okay – you wanna talk – let's talk..."

"Can we go talk in private?"

"Cyn – I'll see you later..."

"You sure?" Mommy asked...

"Yea – I'll call you later..."

"Okay..." Mommy said as she headed to class...

"C'mon..." Chip said as he took Ally's hand...

"Where are we going?"

"You'll see..." Chip said as he took Ally towards the park. When they got to the park, Chip took Ally over by the swings...

"Why are we by the swings?"

"Because I know you like them..."

"Let's go sit on the bench instead..."

"Okay..." Chip said as they both walked over to the bench and sat down...

"I'm sorry..." Chip sighed...

"Sorry for what?"

"I'm sorry for being a dick..." Chip laughed...

"It's not funny!"

"I know..." he said as he took her hand...

"Why are we here Chip?"

"Can we start over?"

"You wanna start over?"

"Yes..."

"Do you love me?"

"I guess..."

"If you have to guess – you know what – this was a waste of time – I never should've come here..." Ally said as she got up to leave...

"No Ally – wait – I love you – I was just stupid..."

"That's true..."

"I deserve that..."

"That's true too..."

"Ally – I wanna be there for you... and the baby..."

"You mean it?"

"Yes..."

"Be there how?"

"Let's get married..."

"What did you just say?"

"I said..." he said as he got down on bended knee and opened a box... "Let's get married..."

"Oh Chip – you mean it?"

"Yes Ally..."

"Oh Chip – I love you so much!" Ally whispered as she started crying...

"I love you too..." he said as he put the ring on her finger...

"Good morning..." Ronald Answered...

"Ronald – this is Phillip – how are ya?"

"I'm good Phillip – how are you?"

"I'm very happy we're going to be grandparents..."

"I beg your pardon?"

"We're going to be grandparents..."

"I don't understand..."

"Ally's my daughter..."

"Ooohhh... – I didn't know that..."

"Small world – Isn't it?"

"That it is – that it is..."

"I'll guess you'll be coming to see me soon..."

"Do I have an appointment?"

"Not yet... but I figured you might want to update your will now that you have a grandchild on the way..."

"Phillip – I have another call – I'll get back to you..." Ronald said and then he hung up abruptly...

"I bet..." Phillip laughed...

"Hey Dad..." Chip said as he walked in...

"Hey..."

"Can we talk?"

"Sure..." Chip walked into the library and closed the door...

"I fixed it..."

"You're back on the team?"

"Yes..."

"How'd you do it?"

"I went to talk to the coach – he didn't want to give me another chance at first – but I asked him what I need to do to fix it..."

"What'd he say?"

"He said it was your job – not his..."

"What the fuck is that supposed to mean?"

"He said he shouldn't have to tell me how to be a man..."

"Mutha fucka..."

"Dad – he's right..."

"Oh so I didn't teach you how to be a man?"

"Yes you did – so I had a talk with Ally, I asked her if we could start over, I told her I wanted to be there for her and the baby... and..."

"And what?"

"I asked her to marry me Dad..."

"I see..."

"Is that all you have to say?"

"What would you like me to say Chip?"

"You could congratulate me..."

"I could... but I'm not..."

"Why?"

"Last week you didn't want anything to do with the girl – you came crying to me – I wrote her a check to go get an abortion – now all of a sudden you wanna marry her..."

"Dad – I'm just trying to do the right thing..."

"I'm not so sure this is the right thing..."

"Isn't that what you did with Mom?"

"That's exactly what I did with your mother..."

"Did you love Mom?"

"Absolutely..."

"I'm going to talk to Mom..." Chip sighed as he went to find his mother...

"Mom, can we talk?"

"Sure..." she answered as she sat down on the couch... "Talk to me..." she said as she took Chip's hand...

"I asked Ally to marry me..."

"Are you sure you wanna get married?"

"I'm just trying to do the right thing..."

"Do you love Ally? Be honest..."

"Kinda..."

"What does that mean?"

"I'm not in love with her – but I love her..."

"Marriage is a huge commitment – you can't just do it because it's convenient..."

"Mom?"

"Yes Chip..."

"Do you love Dad?"

"Yes..."

"Does he love you?"

"Don't you think you should be asking him that?" she laughed...

"I mean... do you think he loves you?"

"Why are you asking me this?"

"You hit Dad..."

"Is that what this is about?" she laughed...

"Well... yea..."

"Your father told you he was going to slap the shit outta me..."

"I know..."

"It was disrespectful..."

"Has Dad ever hit you?"

"No..."

"I hope I never hit Ally..."

"You better not..." she laughed...

"I hope Ally never hits me either..." Chip laughed...

"I don't think you'll have to worry about that..."

"I'm gonna be a Dad..." he sighed...

"Yes you are..."

"Are you mad at me?"

"Am I mad at you? For what?"

"For getting Ally pregnant..."

"I'm not mad – Ally's a nice girl – she's carrying my grandchild – and you're getting married..."

"Yea..."

Mommy and Daddy were all smiles as they walked on the stage together. Today was their high school graduation day and my Grandma's and Grandpa's were right in the front row...

"It gives me great pleasure to announce that this year we have two valedictorians!" the principal boomed through the microphone... "Ryan Davis... and Cynthia Lawrence!"

"Yeeaaa!"

"Woo Hoo!"

"Whistle!"

"Clap!"

"Ryan and Cynthia – please step up to the podium..." the principal said. Everyone got quiet as Mommy and Daddy came up to the podium. My Grandmas and Grandpas took out their cameras and started taking pictures as my Dad spoke first...

"Class of 2020 – we made it!" Daddy exclaimed...

"Yeeaaa!"

"Woo Hoo!"

"Whistle!"

"Clap!"

"We made it – but this is just the beginning of our journey. We need to keep up the momentum we have and use it to propel us into the future – because our lives depend on it..."

"Yeeaaa!"

"Woo Hoo!"

"Whistle!"

"Clap!" When Mommy went over to the microphone to speak, everyone got quiet again...

"Class of 2020 – this year we had a lot of highs – but we also had a lot of lows – and we had many challenges – but we didn't let that stop us..."

"Yeeaaa!"

"Woo Hoo!"

"Whistle!"

"Clap!"

"We are here as proof that we're in this together and we can do anything we put our minds to!"

"Yeeaaa!"

"Woo Hoo!"

"Whistle!"

"Clap!"

"Mom, Dad, Principals, and Professors – thank you for everything you did to help get us here – and keep us here..."

"Yeeaaa!"

"Woo Hoo!"

"Whistle!"

"Clap!" Mommy stepped away from the microphone and everyone got quiet as Daddy stepped up to speak...

"Mom, Dad, Principals, and Professors – in addition to thanking you I wanna thank the coaches and my teammates!"

"Yeeaaa!"

"Woo Hoo!"

"Whistle!"

"Clap!"

"I have a special announcement to make..." Daddy said as he took Mommy by the hand and she stood next to him... "Last week I proposed to Cyn – and she said yes!"

"Yeeaaa!"

"Woo Hoo!"

"Whistle!"

"Clap!" Everyone stood up and continued clapping as Mommy and Daddy left the stage. When they got down off the stage, there were so many people hugging Mommy and Daddy, Mommy started getting dizzy...

"Cyn – are you alright?" Bri asked...

"Yea – I'm just a little light headed..."

"C'mon – let's go get you something to eat..." Bri said as Mommy, Daddy, my Grandmas, and my Grandpas said their goodbyes and left...

"Okay Cyn – what do you have a taste for?" Robert asked..."

"Italian..."

"I'm making lasagna on Sunday – can we have something else?"

"Okay – how about Chinese?"

"Great – we can do Hibachi..."

"Hibachi?"

"That's where they cook the food in front of you..." Daddy said...

"Okay!" Mommy squealed as they started walking towards the car...

"Cyn! Wait up!" Ally called out. Everybody waited for Cyn to catch up...

"Hi Ally, Hi Chip..." Mommy said...

"Hello..." Chip said... "Mom, Dad – this is Ryan, his parents, and his fiancée..."

"Hi Ryan, hi parents, hi fiancée – nice to meet you..." Ronald said as everybody laughed...

"We're going for Hibachi – why don't you join us?"

"Fine with me..." Regina said...

"Okay..." Ronald said...

"You goin' to Ichiro in Trumbull?" Phillip asked...

"Yea – is that okay?" Robert asked...

"I love Ichiro..." Alice said...

"Good – 'cause I'm hungry!" Bri laughed...

"Okay – we'll follow you..." Ronald said and then everybody got in their cars and headed to the restaurant...

Chapter Eighteen

"Welcome to Ichiro – how many?"

"Twelve..." Robert answered...

"We have one table left – right this way..." the hostess said as everyone followed her. Once they were seated, Robert spoke first...

"Hello everyone – I'm Robert, this is my wife Bri, and this is our daughter, Cyn...

"I'm Joshy, this is my husband Ryan, and this is our son, Ryan..."

"I'm Ronald, this is my wife Regina, and this is our son Chip..."

"I'm Alice, this is my husband Phillip, and this is our daughter Ally..."

"Congratulations on your engagement..." Phillip said...

"Thank you..." Mommy and Daddy said in unison...

"Speaking of engagements..." Chip said as he took Ally's hand... "I asked Ally to marry me... and she said yes..."

"Oh my God! Ally! I'm so happy for you!" Mommy squealed as she jumped up from the table, Ally jumped up, they ran to each other... hugged... and cried. Bri, Alice, and Regina took out their cell phones and took pictures...

"Why didn't you tell me?" Mommy asked...

"He just proposed yesterday..."

"Hmmm... congratulations Chip..." Daddy said...

"Thanks Ryan..." Chip sighed...

"Hello everyone – can I start you off with something to drink?" the hostess asked as she gave everyone menus...

"Ginger ale for me..." Mommy answered...

"Pepsi for me..." Daddy answered...

"How about a pitcher of ginger ale and a pitcher of Pepsi?" the hostess asked...

"That'll work..." Robert answered...

"Moscato will work for me..." Bri said...

"That'll work for me too..." Alice said...

"Me too..." Regina said...

"Me four..." Joshy laughed...

"I'll have an O'Doul's..." Robert said...

"I'll have a Coors..." Ronald said...

"I'll have a Guinness..." Phillip said...

"I'll have a Corona..." Ryan said...

"Okay – I'll be back..." the hostess said as she walked away...

"Wow – let's look at this menu..." Alice said as she opened it. Everybody opened their menus and Mommy spoke... "I want chicken & shrimp with fried rice..." she said as the hostess came back with the wine... "I'll be back..." she said...

"I see she got the wine right..." Ronald laughed...

"Absolutely..." Alice said as she sipped her wine...

"Here's your soda..." the hostess said as she put the pitchers on the table...

"That wine looks good..." Ally said...

"Here's Your O'Doul's, Guinness, Corona, and Coors..." the hostess said as she put the drinks on the table...

"Okay - what's everybody having?" she asked...

"Chicken & shrimp with fried rice..." Mommy answered...

"Okay – I'm going to go around the table to the right – next?"

"Chicken & steak..."

"Chicken & salmon..."

"Lobster & steak..."

"Chicken & salmon..."

"Lobster & steak..."

"Lobster & steak..."

"Steak & salmon..."

"Shrimp & scallops..."

"Steak & shrimp..."

"Steak & scallops..."

"Steak & Seabass..."

"Got it – the chef will be out in a moment..." she said as she took the order back to the chef. The chef came over with the cart, heated up the cooking station, and asked if anybody wanted Saki...

"Oh no, no thank you..." everyone said...

"Okay then – everybody want fried rice?"

"Yes..." they all answered in unison...

"Good – we do salad first..." he said as he began giving everyone salad bowls. Mommy started eating the salad and I didn't like the ginger dressing...

"Uh oh..." Mommy said as she rubbed her stomach..."

"What's wrong Cyn?" Daddy asked...

"Oh God..." Mommy groaned as she jumped up and ran to the bathroom with Daddy right behind her...

"Cyn – are you alright?" Daddy asked as he heard Mommy heaving into the toilet...

"I don't think our Christmas Miracle likes ginger dressing..." Mommy laughed...

"Is the alright?" Alice asked...

"She's pregnant..." Bri answered...

"I'm not looking forward to that..." Ally said...

"I don't know why they call it morning sickness..." Regina laughed...

"I know – it should be called morning, noon, and night sickness..." Joshy laughed...

"You alright?" Bri asked as Mommy and Daddy came back to the table...

"I'm okay Mommy..."

"Good – 'cause I'm ready to eat..." Bri laughed...

"Everybody ready?" the chef asked...

"Ready!" they all answered in unison...

"Here you go..." he said as he gave everyone shrimp..."

"No thank you..." Daddy said...

"I want it!" Mommy exclaimed...

"Okay – extra shrimp for you!" the chef said as everyone laughed...

"How many weeks are you?" Alice asked...

"Twelve weeks..."

"Oh so you're having a Christmas baby..." Regina said...

"Yes she is – she's been calling the baby her Christmas Miracle..." Bri said...

"What if it's a boy?" Chip asked...

"Well then – he'll be our Christmas Miracle..." Daddy answered...

"I'm not a boy – I'm a girl!" I exclaimed as if they could hear me...

"Here ya go..." the chef said as he put the fried rice on everyone's plates...

"Ooohhh... this looks so good..." Ally said as she tasted it...

"How many are you Ally?" Joshy asked...

"Two weeks..."

"Aww..." Bri said...

"So is everyone going to Harvard?" Ronald asked as the chef put the noodles on everyone's plates...

"I am..." Daddy answered...

"So am I..." Mommy answered...

"So am I..." Ally answered as the chef put vegetables on everyone's plate...

"Are you going to college right away Ryan?" Phillip asked...

"I'm not sure yet..." Daddy answered...

"You can't let me go by myself..." Chip said as the chef put the shrimp, chicken, salmon, lobster, steak, scallops, and seabass on everyone's plates...

"Aww... I love you too Chip..." Daddy said as everyone laughed...

"More wine?" the hostess asked...

"Yes please..." Bri answered...

"Me too..." Joshy, Alice, and Regina said in unison and then they all laughed. Everyone continued eating as the hostess brought more wine...

"More beer?"

"Yes Maam!" Robert exclaimed...

"Okay – I'll be right back..." the hostess said as she went to get the beers...

"Ryan – can I talk to you a minute?" Chip asked...

"Sure – excuse us..." Daddy said as they both got up and left the table. Daddy followed Chip out into the lobby and Chip spoke...

"I got us a room..."
"Us?"
"Me and Ally..."
"Ooohhh..."
"I need your advice..."
"Okay..."
"The first time was really awkward..."
"Oh my God – you were a virgin!"
"Will you keep your voice down?!"
"Sorry about that..."
"Anyway – what should I do?"
"Just take your time..."
"Is that it?"
"If you're really excited – don't pump fast – take it slow..."
"Okay – anything else?"
"You'll be fine... Daddy said...
"Thanks..."
"C'mon – let's get back in there..." Daddy said...

"You guys good?" Phillip asked as they sat back down...
"We're good..." Chip asked...
"You guys wanna get the check?" Ronald asked...

"Oh no – that's okay..." Daddy answered as everybody laughed...

"Any dessert?" the hostess asked...

"None for me..." Mommy said...

"Anybody else?" the hostess asked...

"Oh no..." Everyone answered...

"Okay then – I'll be back with the check..." the hostess said as she went to get the check...

"This was really nice – thank you for joining us..." Robert said...

"Thank you for having us..." Alice said...

"We're getting together for dinner on Sunday – would you all like to come have dinner with us? I'm cooking..."

"Okay!" Alice exclaimed...

"As long as I can watch the game..." Phillip said...

"I'll bring Moscato..." Regina said...

"I'll bring my appetite..." Ronald said as everyone laughed...

"Here's your check..." the hostess said as she placed the check on the table...

"I got it..." Ronald said...

"Thank you..." Robert said...

"Thank you..." Ryan said...

"Thank you..." Phillip said...

"You're welcome – we need to get going – c'mon Regina..."

"Chip – are you coming?" Regina asked...

"No Mom..."

"Okay – nice meeting you all – see you Sunday..." Regina said as they left...

"I guess they're in a hurry..." Joshy laughed...

"I guess so..." Alice laughed...

"We might as well get going too..." Robert said as he got up...

"What's your hurry?" Bri asked as they all laughed...

"C'mon..." Phillip said as he got up and Alice got up with him...

"I'm going with Chip..." Ally sighed...

"We know..." Phillip laughed...

"We'll see you later..." Robert said as he got up and Bri got up with him...

"Okay – bye..." Mommy said...

"C'mon Ally – let's go..." Chip said as he got up...

"Okay – I'll call you later Cyn..." she said as she got up and they left..."

"C'mon – I have a surprise for you..." Daddy said as he got up...

"Okay – I'm coming..." Mommy said as she got up and then they left...

"Ronald – I'm sorry – I shouldn't've slapped you..."

"Shut the fuck up!" Ronald growled as he slammed the door and locked it. Regina stood there in shock with her eyes wide open... "Get your ass over here..." he commanded as he smiled at her mischievously...

"Yes Daddy..." she breathed as she went over to him, he grabbed her around her waist, and he kissed her hard...

"I could get used to this..." Alice sighed as Phillip closed the door behind them and locked it...

"So could I..." Phillip breathed as he pushed Alice up against the door and pressed himself up against her...

"Phillip... she breathed as he kissed her hard and pushed his tongue in her mouth...

"Come with me..." Ryan breathed as he pulled Joshy into their son's room...

"Ryan..." Joshy breathed as he pushed her down on the bed... "We can't..."

"Yes..." Ryan breathed as he got on top of Joshy and started kissing her... "We can..."

"Ryan... wait..."

"No..."

"What... if... he... finds... out?"

"I won't tell... if you don't..." he breathed as he took his dick out his pants...

"Come with me..." Robert said as he took Bri into the library, closed the door, and locked it. Robert went over to the couch, sat down, opened his pants, and took his dick out... "Come say hello to your favorite guy..." he said as he waived his dick at Bri. Bri went over to the couch, stood in front of Robert, and lifted her dress. Robert smiled when he saw she wasn't wearing any panties...

Ronald led Regina into the dining room, turned her around, and bent her down on the table... "Ronald!" she gasped as he lifted her dress, ripped her panties off, and slammed his dick inside her...

"Yes... that's it..." he growled as he began pounding her...

"Ronald... Ronald... Oh God... Yessss..."

Phillip slid his hand up under Alice's dress and ripped her panties off... "Oh Phillip!" she moaned as Phillip lifted her legs and she wrapped them around his back as he slammed his dick inside her...

"Ryan... Ryan... Ryan..."

"Joshy... Joshy... Joshy..."

"I'm cumming Ryan... I'm cumming..."

"I'm cumming with you Baby..."

"Uuugh! Uuugh! Uuugh! Uuugh! Uuugh!

"Aagh! Aagh! Aagh! Aagh! Aagh!"

"Oh God... Robert..."

"That's it Bri... ride my dick..."

"Harder Robert..."

"You like that?"

"Yes Robert... Yes... Yes... I'm cumming!"

"Cum for me Baby..."

"Huh... Huh... Huh... Huh... Huh..." Robert pushed Bri down on the couch while he was still inside her and began pounding her...

"Shit... I'm about to cum..." Ronald grunted...

"I'm cummin'... I'm cummin'... I'm cummin'..."

"Uuugh! Uuugh! Uuugh! Uuugh! Uuugh!"

"Haagh! Haagh! Haagh! Haagh! Haagh!"

"Oh Phillip... Don't stop..."

"I won't... I won't..."

"Oh yes... That's it... Right there..."

"Alice... Alice... Alice... I'm cummin'..."

"Cum with me Phillip..."

"Uuugh! Uuugh! Uuugh! Uuugh! Uuugh!"

"Aagh! Aagh! Aagh! Aagh! Aagh!"

"Oh Ryan... that was so good..."

"Yes Baby... Yes..."

"We better get up..."

"I don't wanna stop..."

"I don't wanna get caught...

"Please Baby... Don't make me stop...

"Robert!" Bri screamed as he pounded her...

"Uuugh! Uuugh! Uuugh! Uuugh Uuugh!"

"I'm... Cummin'... Again... Aaagh! Aaagh! Aaagh! Aaagh! Aaagh!"

"Damn..." Ronald breathed as he lay down on Regina's back...

"If this is what I get for slapping you..." she panted... "I'm gonna slap you more often..."

"Oh Phillip..." Alice breathed...

"Yes Alice... Yes..." he breathed as he kissed her...

"I've never seen you like this..." she breathed...

"I really enjoyed that..." he breathed...

"So did I..." she breathed...

"I'm cummin' Baby... I'm cummin..." Ryan moaned...

"I'm cummin' with you..."

"Uuugh! Uuugh! Uuugh! Uuugh! Uuugh!"

"Aaagh! Aaagh! Aaagh! Aaagh! Aaagh!"

"We better get up now..." Ryan breathed as he kissed Joshy...

"Okay..."

"Damn that was good..." Robert breathed...

"Hell yea..." Bri breathed...

"You weren't wearing any panties..." he breathed as he kissed her...

"I know..."

"I wish I had known that earlier..."

"I'm glad you didn't...

"Why's that?"

"I might not have been able to wait until we got home..."

"Oh Wow..." Ally said as they pulled up to the Holiday Inn...

"Surprise..." Chip said. Ally didn't say anything... "Are you okay?"

"I guess..." she sighed...

"C'mon..." he said as he opened the door and got out the car. Ally didn't get out so he went and opened the door for her... "You comin'?" he asked as he extended his hand for her to take...

"I'm coming..." she sighed as she took his hand. The valet parked the car and they went inside...

"Welcome to the Holiday Inn..." the clerk said...

"I'm here to check in..." Chip said...

"Name please?"

"Chip Stuart..."

"Hold on a minute..." she said as she looked up the reservation on the computer... "You're all set..." she said as she handed him the room keys...

"Thanks..." Chip said as he took the keys, took Ally by the hand, and walked her to the elevator...

"What floor is the room on?"

"It's on the 3rd floor..." Chip answered as the elevator doors opened and he took Ally in the elevator...

"I've never been here..." Ally said...

"We can go to Park City Grill later... if you're hungry..."

"3rd floor..." Ally said as the elevator stopped and the doors opened...

"C'mon – I wanna show you something..." Chip said as he took Ally's hand...

"Okay..." Chip took Ally's hand and led her down the hall... "Surprise..." he said as she came around the corner...

"Ooohhh... they have a pool..."

"Yea..."

"I don't have a bathing suit..." she laughed nervously...

"You don't need one..."

"You want us to swim naked?"

"Oh my God!" Chip laughed... "Ally – look!" Ally looked in the pool and saw a couple swimming in their shorts and t-shirts...

"Oh my God..." she laughed... "I can't believe I thought you wanted us to swim naked..." she laughed...

"I do..." he whispered... but not out here..."

"Ooohhh..."

"You ready to go to the room?"

"Okay..." she said as she took Chips hand. When they got to the room, Chip opened the door, Ally followed him inside, and then she looked around the room as Chip put the Do Not Disturb sign on the door before locking it...

"You like it?"

"Yea..." Chip walked over to Ally, took her in his arms, and kissed her...

"Chip... wait..."

"Okay... I'll wait..." Ally sat on the bed and Chip sat beside her...

"I don't wanna have sex..."

"Really?"

"I wanna make love..."

"We can do that..." Chip said as they started kissing again...

"I love you Chip..."

"I love you too..." he breathed as he laid her down on the bed and they continued kissing...

"I thought I lost you..."

"I'm sorry I hurt you..."

"How much time do we have?"

"You wanna leave?" Chip laughed...

"No..."

"We have all night..."

"Really?"

"I have a confession to make..."

"You've been with someone else?"

"No..."

"What then?" Ally said as she stopped kissing him...

"It was my first time too..." he breathed as he pulled her back into a kiss...

"I thought so..."

"You did?"

"Yea..."

"Was it that obvious?"

"Yea..."

"I'm about to make up for it..." he said as he sat up and took off his shirt. Ally sat up and Chip took her blouse off over her head... "Now for dessert..." he said as he unhooked her bra, slid it off, and tossed it. Chip leaned forward and began sucking on her breast...

"Ooohhh..."

"You like that?" he asked as he flicked his tongue on her nipple and grabbed the other breast in his hand...

"Yea..." she panted...

"Lay down..." he commanded. Ally lay down and Chip took her other breast in his mouth and began sucking it...

"Oh Chip..." Ally moaned as Chip played with her other breast. Chip moved his hand down her stomach to her pants and opened them as he continued sucking her breast... "Oh...

Chip..." she moaned. Chip put his hand inside her pants, found her clit, and began swirling his fingers around it... "Chip... Huh... Chip..." Chip put two fingers inside her and moved them in and out as he began sucking on her other breast... "Ooohhh... Chip... I'm gonna cum... I'm gonna cum... Huh... Huh... Huh..."

"Cum for me Ally..." Chip breathed as he flicked his tongue on her nipple and continued moving his fingers in and out of her...

"HUH... HUH... HUH... HUH..."

"Was that better?" he breathed as he continued licking and sucking on her breasts...

"Yea..." Ally panted...

"Good..." Chip said as he got up on his knees, took his pants and boxers off, and lay back down next to her. Ally got up, took her pants and panties off, got back on the bed, laid down next to Chip, and took his penis in her hands... "Ally..." Chip panted...

"Come here..." Ally commanded as she pulled him to her and began kissing him as she stroked his penis...

"Ally... Ohh... Ally... I'm gonna cum... I can't hold it..."

"Cum for me..." Ally breathed and then she kissed him hard...

"Ooohhh... Ooohhh... Ooohhh... Uuuggghhh!" Ally rubbed Chip's ejaculate all over his penis... "Ally – stop..."

"Why?"

"I'm a mess..." he laughed...

"So am I..." she laughed...

"I'm glad we have all night... I'm gonna need it..."

"No... you won't..." Ally said as she continued playing with his penis...

"Oohhh... your hand feels good..."

"You like this?"

"Yea..."

"You're getting hard again..."

"I know..." Chip panted...

"Get on top..." Ally commanded as she got on her back and opened her legs. Chip got on top and eased himself inside her and began kissing her...

"Mmm... Mmm... Mmm..."

"Mmmph... Mmmph... Mmmph..."

"Mmm... Mmm... Mmm..."

"Mmmph... Mmmph... Mmmph..."

"Mmm... Mmm... Mmm..."

"Mmmph... Mmmph... Mmmph..."

"Mmm... Mmm... Mmm..."

"Mmmph... Mmmph... Mmmph..."

"Mmm... Mmm... Mmm..."

"Mmmph... Mmmph... Mmmph..."

"MMM!... MMM!... MMM!..."

"MMMPH!... MMMPH!... MMMPH!..."

"Where are we going?" Mommy asked...

"You'll see..." Daddy answered. Mommy kept looking out the window as Daddy drove.

After they got to City Hall, Daddy drove into the parking lot, parked the car, and turned off the ignition...

“Ryan?”

“Yes Cyn?”

“What are we doing here?” Daddy turned to face Mommy and took her hand...

“Cyn... I want us to go get our marriage license...”

“You want us to do that now?”

“Yes – I wanna have it so we can show it to our parents on Sunday...”

“Oh Ryan... I love you...”

“I love you too... and I wanna marry you as soon as possible...

“You wanna elope?”

“Our parent’s would never forgive us if we did that...” Daddy laughed...

“Okay – let’s go!” Mommy squealed as they both got out the car and hurried inside...

“Good afternoon…” the clerk said… “How may I help you?”

“We’re here to get our marriage license…” Daddy said as he smiled…

“Aww… congratulations…”

“Thank you…”

“Do you have valid identification?”

“What do you mean?”

“If you have identification from the Department of Motor Vehicles that’ll be sufficient

– otherwise, I'll need another form of identification and your birth certificate…"

"We have valid identification…" Daddy said as he took out his driver's license and handed it to her...

"May I have your ID please?" she asked Mommy…

"Sure…" Mommy said as Mommy handed the clerk her driver's license…

"I need to make a copy of these to attach to your application – I'll be right back…" she said as she walked over to the copy machine. Mommy and Daddy looked at each other and smiled…

"Here ya go…" the clerk said as she gave us back our licenses…

"I need you both to fill this out completely – once you fill it out – I'll look it over, make sure it's filled out properly, and then we'll all sign it…"

"Okay…" Daddy said as he took the form and began filling it out. Mommy waited patiently as he filled out his side, but Mommy wanted him to hurry up so she could fill out her side…

"Here, here!" Daddy laughed as he gave it to Mommy. Mommy studied his side and then started filling out her side with her name, date of birth, social security number, etc., and then she filled in her parent's information: Mother – Sabrina Lawrence, Father – Robert Lawrence. Mommy went down the rest of the form and compared her answers to Daddy's: City of Birth – Milford, State – CT, Prior Marriages – No,

Maiden Name – Cynthia Lawrence. When Mommy got to Name on Marriage Certificate – she got another piece of paper and wrote two names: Cynthia Lawrence Davis and Cynthia Davis…

"I like this one…" she said out loud as she wrote Cynthia Davis on the form. After she filled in the name to be put on the Marriage Certificate she checked 'no' where they asked for preference to hyphenate the name. Mommy saw Daddy's signature at the bottom of the form and she started crying after she signed her name…

"Aww…" the clerk said as she handed Mommy tissues…

"Sorry…" Mommy laughed…

"Don't ever apologize for happiness…" the clerk said as she took the form and read it over…

"Ryan?" she asked…

"Yes?"

"Did you fill this out of your own free will?"

"Yes Maam…"

"Is this your signature?" she asked as she pointed to Daddy's signature…

"Yes Maam…"

"Cynthia?"

"Yes?"

"Did you fill this out of your own free will?"

"Yes Maam!"

"Is this your signature?" she asked as she pointed to Mommy's signature…

"Yes Maam!"

"Okay..." she laughed... "I'm going to process this and get you your license – once I do that – you can get married anytime you want – but you have to get married within 60 days – if you don't get married in within 60 days it will expire – and you'll be back to see me... I'll be right back..." she said as she went into the office behind the counter...

"I love you Ryan..."

"I love you too..." Daddy said and then he kissed Mommy...

"Here's your license..." the clerk said as she handed Mommy and Daddy their license. They looked at the license, and then they looked at each other...

"Do you have any questions?" Mommy looked at their license again and read the signature at the bottom:

Prepared by: Alberta Woody
Title: City Clerk
City: Milford
State: CT

"No..." Mommy sighed...

"Do you have any questions Ryan?"

"No Maam..."

"On your wedding day – give this license to the wedding officiant – they'll sign it, date it, and then they'll mail it out to Vital Records for the state you get married in and a copy of it will also be sent here. You'll receive your Marriage Certificate from the Vital Records Office…"

"Thank you Ms. Woody…" Mommy said as she gave her a hug…"

"You can call me Alberta…" she said as she pulled Mommy and Daddy into a hug and started crying…

"You okay?" Daddy asked…

"I'm fine – I'm just happy…" she said as she wiped her eyes…"

"Aww… we're happy too… right Cyn?"

"Yes sir!" Mommy yelled so loud everyone in the office bust out laughing... "I'm getting married!" Mommy yelled from the top of the steps as soon as they stepped outside. People in the street stopped and applauded while Mommy and Daddy held each other and kissed. They were blocking the entrance but everyone was happy for them so they just waited until Mommy and Daddy stopped kissing…

"I'm so happy…" Mommy cried…

"So am I..." Daddy cried...

Chapter TWENTY-ONE

"I can't believe you invited them to dinner today..." Bri sighed...

"Are you upset with me?" Robert asked...

"No – I just wish you would've asked me first..."

"I'm sorry..." he said as he pulled her into a kiss... "I invited them in the moment – Cyn was so happy..."

"She was happy..."

"So you forgive me?"

"As long as I don't have to wash the dishes..." she laughed as there was a knock on the door...

"I'll get it!" Mommy yelled as she hurried downstairs... "Hi Ryan!" Mommy beamed when she saw Daddy...

"Hi Cyn!" Daddy exclaimed as he picked Mommy up and kissed her...

"Hi – remember us?" Joshy laughed...

"Hi Joshy..." Bri laughed...

"C'mon on in Ryan..." Robert laughed...

"We're gonna have some fun today..." Ryan laughed...

"Is that right?" Robert asked...

"Oh yea – Phillip's a fan of dem Cowboys..." Ryan laughed

"Oh my God – they're playing Washington today – I can't wait!" Robert laughed...

"Who is it?" Bri asked as she went to the door...

"It's Regina..." she answered...

"Hi Regina, Hi Ronald, Hi Chip – come on in..." Bri said...

"Hi Ron, Regina – Chip, Cyn and Ryan are in there somewhere...

"Hi Mr. Lawrence – thanks!" Chip said as he hurried into the living room...

"Hey Chip..." Daddy said...

"Hey Chip..." Mommy said...

"Hey guys..." Chip said...

"C'mon ladies – we'll go sit in the dining room..." Bri said as they followed her into the dining room...

"Where's that moscato you promised?" Bri laughed...

"Right here!" Regina laughed as she took it out the gift bag...

"I'll get glasses..." Bri said as she got up...

"We're drinking already?" Joshy asked...

"You know today's Sunday – right?" Bri asked...

"Yea? So?" Regina asked...

"So... the Cowboys are playing today..." Bri answered...

"Oh my God!" Regina laughed...

"Oh so you know what I'm talking about!" Bri laughed...

"Oh yea – my husband's volume goes up ten-fold when the Cowboys are playing!" Regina laughed...

"Is he a fan?" Joshy asked...

"Hell no!" Regina laughed...

"You watch the game?" Bri asked...

"I love them Patriots!" Regina exclaimed...

"My husband loves the Patriots..." Joshy said...

"My husband's a 49er fan – but he's also a fan of the game..." Bri said...

"You watch the game?" Regina asked...

"I watch once in a while to keep him company... but I don't get into it like he does..." Bri laughed as she poured the wine...

"I sure hope we have some wine left for dinner..." Regina laughed...

"If we don't – we'll just send the kids to get more..." Bri laughed...

"Mom – Ally's here!" Mommy called out...

"Hi everyone!" Alice said as she walked into the dining room and placed a bottle of moscato on the table...

"Oh thank God!" Regina laughed...

"What's so funny?" Alice asked...

"The Cowboys are playing..." Regina answered...

"Ooohhhh..." Alice said as they all laughed...

"Phillip – join us..." Robert said...

"How's everybody doing?" Phillip asked...

"We're all good now – the question is – how will you be doing later?" Robert asked as Ryan and Ronald laughed...

"I'll be doing just fine..." Phillip answered sarcastically as they laughed...

"I hope you don't have money on the game..." Robert laughed...

"If I put money on it – I'd put my money on Washington..." Phillip laughed...

"And that's when Dallas will win!" Ryan laughed...

"How long before dinner's ready?" Joshy asked...

"Hungry already?" Bri asked...

"Not at all – I just wanna know how much time we have to ourselves..." Joshy laughed...

"I know – I can't wait for Chip to go to college – I feel like I have a curfew..." Regina laughed...

"Oh my God – Ally's the same way – Mommy – where you goin' – what time you comin' back – I don't wanna be here by myself!" Alice laughed...

"I don't have to worry about that with Cyn – either she's with Ryan or on the phone with him..." Bri laughed...

"Cyn – I need to talk to you..." Ally said...

"Okay – c'mon – let's go upstairs..." Mommy said as they left the living room...

"I'm glad they left..." Chip said...

"Why?" Ryan asked...

"Cause I need to talk to you too..."

"Okay – tell me..." Mommy whispered as they sat down...

"Cyn... oh my God..." Ally sighed...

"You had sex again!" Mommy exclaimed...

"Yeeesss..."

"It was good?"

"It was great..."

"I'm so happy for you..." Mommy said as they hugged...

"I'm glad I'm going to college with Chip..." Ally said...

"You're going to stay on campus with him?"

"He's moving to Cambridge... and I'm going with him..."

"He's getting his own place?"

"Yea..."

"Oh so you can have sex whenever you want!" Mommy exclaimed...

"Yea..."

"I wish we could do that – we're gonna have to move in with Ryan's parents..." Mommy sighed...

"Oh no..."

"That's what I'm saying – his parents are great – but I won't be comfortable having sex in their house – even after we get married..."

"Why? You're already pregnant – they know you're having sex..."

"I don't want them to hear us..." Mommy laughed...

"What happened?" Daddy asked...

"Remember I told you I got us a room..."

"Yea – I remember..."

"Well...."

"How was it?"

"Let's just say... I redeemed myself..." Chip said as he smiled...

"I'm happy for you Chip..."

"I'm happy too..."

"So you don't have any regrets about asking her to marry you?"

"No..."

"Are you sure you're ready for this? You know you like to play around..."

"I don't wanna do that anymore. I love Ally..."

"You love Ally? Since when?"

"I'm not in love with her – but I love her..."

"Does she know that?"

"She knows I love her..."

"Don't hurt her Chip..."

"I'm not..."

"When are you getting married?"

"I don't know yet..."

"Are your parents going to let her move in with you or vice-versa until you get married?"

"We won't have to worry about that..."

"Really?"

"I'm moving to Cambridge so I can be on campus in September... and Ally's coming with me..."

"You're going to have your own place?"

"Yea..."

"Congratulations..." Daddy sighed...

"What's wrong?"

"We have to move in with my parents..."

"Oooohhh..."

"Don't get me wrong – my parents are great – but I'm not going to feel comfortable having sex with my parents in the house..."

"Why not – Cyn's already pregnant..."

"I don't want them to hear us making noise..."

"Is Cyn a screamer?"

"Oh no..."

"Well then – as soon as she starts moaning just kiss her – it'll muffle her moans..."

"How do you know that?"

"My father told me he used to do that when girls would sneak him in their room..."

"Oh my God – your father had sex with girls in their house? When their parents were home?"

"Yea..." Chip laughed...

"Dinner's ready!" Bri called out...

"Coming!" Mommy yelled and she and Ally hurried downstairs...

"C'mon..." Daddy said as he got up and Chip followed him into the dining room...

"Let's go..." Robert said as Ryan, Ronald, and Phillip followed him into the dining room...

"Mom – you need any help?" Daddy asked...

"Sit down Bri – we'll get it..." Robert said as he got up and Daddy followed him into the kitchen. They got plates, forks, two spatulas, and brought them into the dining room...

"I got it..." Chip said as he got up and set the table. Robert and Daddy went back into the kitchen, took 4 trays of lasagna out the oven, and put them on the table one by one. After they put the lasagna on the table, they went back into the kitchen, got the salad and the garlic bread, and put that on the table too...

"You cooked all this?" Ryan asked...

"I did..." Robert answered...

"I love a man that can cook!" Regina said...

"Amen!" Alice agreed. Daddy and Robert went back into the kitchen, took out two pitchers of sweet tea, brought them into the dining room, and placed them on the table...

"Ooohhh... I love sweet tea..." Ally sighed as Daddy and Robert went back into the kitchen. Daddy came out with O'Doul's, Coors, Guinness, and Corona...

"Okay – now we ready!" Robert said...

"Thank you Baby..." Bri said...

"Thank you Daddy..." Mommy said...

"You're welcome – now help yourselves!" Robert said as everyone started to eat...

"Mmm... – this is sooo good!" Mommy exclaimed...

"It's good Mommy!" I agreed as I enjoyed it just as much...

"Have you guys set a date yet?" Bri asked...

"Well... I was gonna wait until later to tell you... but since you asked..." Daddy said as he took Mommy's hand... "Cyn... will you marry me... on Monday?"

"You wanna get married tomorrow?" Cyn asked...

"Not tomorrow... next week..."

"Next week? As in Monday, June 28th, four days after we graduate?"

"Yes..."

"Yes Ryan – I'll marry you next week on Monday..." Mommy said and they kissed...

""Wow – that doesn't give us much time to get a dress, get our hair done, our nails done – okay – we'll go to David's Bridal this week – Robert – I need you to..." "Bri..." Robert laughed... we're good – right guys?"

"We're good..." Phillip said...

"We'll coordinate with Robert..." Ronald said...

"Okay good..." Bri continued... "We'll need to get our hair done..."

"Bri – let me know what you need – we gotchu..." Joshy said...

"I'll get us in on Sunday to get our hair done..." Regina said...

"We can go to the spa on Saturday for manicures and pedicures..." Alice said...

"Do you have your marriage license?" Robert asked...

"We have it Daddy..." Mommy answered...

"Have you thought about where you're going to live after you get married?" Bri asked...

"We're going to move in with my parents..." Daddy answered...

"Oh so you've decided?" Joshy asked...

"Yea..." Daddy answered...

"Okay then!" Ryan said...

"Good – now let's eat, let's drink, and let's go watch dem Cowboys!" Robert said as everyone continued eating...

Chapter Twenty-Two

"Cyn – Ryan's here..." Bri called out...

"C'mon upstairs..." Mommy said...

"Okay!" Daddy exclaimed as he ran upstairs...

"Hi..." Daddy sighed as he picked Mommy up and spun her around...

"Weeee!" I laughed...

"Oh my God – Ryan – give me your hand!"

"Here!" Daddy exclaimed as Mommy snatched Daddy's hand and placed it on her stomach... "Oh my God... is that our baby?" he whispered...

"That's our baby..." Mommy whispered...

"Cyn – can I come in?"

"Come in Mommy..."

"Hey..."

"Mommy – come here..." Mommy said as she took Bri's hand and put it on her stomach...

"Oh my God – she's moving!" Bri exclaimed...

"Yea..." Mommy beamed...

"Robert! Come upstairs!"

"What's wrong?" Robert panted as he came in the room...

"Come here Daddy..." Mommy said as she took Robert's hand and put it on her stomach...

"Hey My Christmas Miracle – you dancin'?" Robert laughed...

"I'm just moving around Grandpa..." I laughed...

"C'mon Ryan – I have something to show you..." Mommy said as she sat in front of the computer. Daddy sat down next to Mommy and Bri and Robert sat down on the edge of the bed...

"Oh you wanna see too?" Mommy laughed...

"Do you mind?" Bri asked...

"No – I need your help..."

"And our money..." Robert laughed...

"I've been looking at the Stonecroft Country Inn..."

"In Ledyard?" Bri asked...

"Yea..." Mommy answered as she pulled it up on the computer...

"It looks romantic..." Robert said...

"It does..." Daddy agreed...

"They have an elopement package..." Mommy said...

"You wanna elope?" Bri asked...

"No... I just like the package..."

"What's in the package?" Robert asked...

"Use of the dining room for two hours, an officiant to perform the ceremony, an hour professional photographer, a Bridal Bouquet, a Groom's Boutonniere, a small wedding cake, champagne, and a one-night stay for the Bride and Groom in either the Sarah or the Shubel room..."

"That sounds nice..." Daddy said...

"It does – but if you want to book it, it only allows you to book three adults..."

"Well – your father's the one that's holding the checkbook – I'll stay home..." Bri laughed...

"Mommy! That's not funny!"

"Cyn – relax – I'll be there..."

"Let's see the rooms..." Daddy said...

"They have 10 rooms..."Mommy said... "This is the Sarah Master Suite..."

"Ooohhh... I like that!" Bri exclaimed...

"So do I..." Robert said as he looked at Bri mischievously...

"Really Dad?" Mommy laughed...

"So that's where we'll be spending our wedding night?" Daddy asked...

"Maybe... maybe not..." Mommy answered...

"What does that mean?" Daddy laughed...

"I like the Shubel Master Suite too..." Mommy said...

"I like that one too..." Bri sighed...

"Your mother and I will stay in that one..." Robert said...

"Robert! We have to wait and see which one they choose..." Bri laughed...

"How many people do you want at your wedding?" Robert asked...

"Just us..." Mommy answered...

"You don't want my parents?" Daddy laughed...

"Of course I want your parents..." Mommy laughed...

"Well... they do have 10 rooms..." Robert said...

"Yes they do..." Mommy said...

"And they have two master suites..." Bri said...

"Well – we're good..." Robert laughed...

"Where would my parents sleep?" Daddy asked...

"I think your parents would love the Stonecroft Room..." Mommy said...

"Ooohhh... Robert – I think I want this room..." Bri said...

"Why can't we have the other room?" Robert laughed...

"This room has a private staircase to the second floor" Mommy said...

"We'll take that one!" Mommy and Daddy said in unison...

"Okay – so they basically have three master suites..." Bri laughed...

"So... you don't want Ally and Chip to come?" Robert asked...

"Well – they have seven rooms left..." Daddy laughed...

"The Orchard Room has a King Feather Bed..." Mommy said...

"Well – I think Ally should get that room..." Bri said...

"What about her parents?" Mommy asked...

"They have six rooms left – I'm sure they're just as nice..." Bri said...

"The other rooms are nice too – they just have queen beds..." Mommy said...

"Let's see 'em..." Daddy said...

"Here they are..." Mommy said...

"Hmmm... they are nice..." Robert said...

"Ally would probably like the Lilly suite..." Mommy said...

"I love the bed in the Briar Rose Suite..." Bri said...

"Ronald would probably like the Orlando Suite..." Robert said...

"Alice would love the Nor'easter Suite..." Bri sighed...

"Do they do weddings for large parties?" Robert asked...

"They do weddings for up to 75 people..." Mommy answered...

"Do they have a menu?" Bri asked...

"They do – but I don't like the food..."

"I'll tell you what – we'll give them a call and see what they can do..." Bri said...

"Thank you Mommy..."

"You could always do a small wedding there, stay there for your wedding night, and have your honeymoon somewhere else..." Robert said...

"That's a good idea..." Daddy said...

"We're gonna be in our room - you let us know what you want..." Bri said as she got up..."

"Okay Mommy..."

"See you later..." Robert said as he got up and left with Bri...

"Finally!" Daddy exclaimed as he got up, pulled Mommy up, and kissed her...

"I wish they'd go out for a while..." Mommy said...

"I miss you..."

"I miss you too- it's driving me crazy..."

"What are we going to do after we get married?"

"I have an idea..."

"You do?"

"Yea – since my Mom's a screamer, we'll just have sex when they do..."

"What if we don't want to?"

"We will... trust me..."

"Why do we have to have sex when your parents have sex? Why can't we have sex whenever we want?"

"Because – if we have sex when my parents are having sex, they won't hear whatever noise we make..."

"Ooohhh..." Mommy laughed...

"Once we move out, we can have sex whenever we want..."

"I wish we could do that now..."

"So do I..."

"Do you think we can make noise on our wedding night?"

"Oh yea..." Daddy breathed as he kissed Mommy on her neck...

"That tickles..." Mommy laughed...

"Honey – c'mere a minute..." Bri said as she looked at their computer...

"What's this?"

"This is the menu from Gourmet Galley..." she explained as Robert sat down next to her...

"Hmmm – let's look at the other menus..."

"Good idea..." Bri said as she pulled up the next one... "A Thyme To Cook..." Bri read out loud...

"Umm... No..." Robert laughed...

"Coastal Gourmet Catering..." Bri read...

"Umm... Is that lobster alive?" Robert asked as he pointed to the picture...

"I hope not..." Bri laughed...

"Let's look at the next one..." Robert laughed...

"Matthew's Catering..." Bri read...

"Oh I like this one already..." Robert breathed...

"Why do we have to go to facebook to see their menus?" Bri asked...

"Cause everybody's in facebook..." Robert laughed...

"Ooohhh. I'm getting hungry looking at their signature selections..." Bri sighed...

"Me too – let's see the next one..."

"Ooohh... look at the Rustic Italian Table..."

"Sold – Next!" Robert laughed...

"Aww... I wish they were getting married at Christmas..." Bri sighed...

"I'm glad they're not..."

"But Honey – they have a Happy Holidays menu..."

"We'll be celebrating the birth of our Christmas Miracle..."

"You're right..."

"I hope they have another name picked out..." Robert laughed...

"Well..." Bri laughed... "At least they can call him or her Chris..." Bri laughed...

"I can live with Chris..."

"Where do you wanna go for our honeymoon?"

"Hawaii..."

"Okay – when you wake up from your dream, let me know where you really wanna go..." Daddy laughed...

"I really wish we could go to Hawaii..." Mommy sighed...

"I wish I could give that to you right now... but I can't..."

"I know..." Mommy sighed...

"Cyn? Ryan? Could you come in here a minute?" Bri called out...

"Coming!" they both answered in unison as they got up and went in the room with Mommy's parents...

"You have a nice room..." Daddy said...

"Thank you..." Robert said...

"Is that a master bathroom?" Daddy asked...

"Yes it is..." Robert answered...

"Can I see it?"

"Why do you wanna see our bathroom?" Bri asked...

"It'll give me an idea of what to look for when we get our own place..." Daddy answered...

"Sure – go 'head..." Robert said. Daddy went into the bathroom and Mommy followed...

"Ooohhh – a walk in shower for two!" Daddy exclaimed...

"Isn't it nice?" Mommy asked...

"You want a soaker tub like that?"

"I won't be able to get in it..." Mommy laughed...

"I'll help you... and then I'll join you..."

"Oh Ryan..." Mommy gushed...

"Two sinks – plenty of counter space for your stuff and mine..."

"Mostly mine though..." Mommy laughed...

"C'mere – I need to show you these menus..." Bri reminded them...

"Sorry Mommy..." Mommy said as they came out the bathroom and went over to the computer...

"We have Matthew's Signature Selections with Appetizers..." Bri said...

"Hmmm... let's see the other one..." Daddy said...

"This is the Rustic Italian Table..." Bri said...

"Sold!" Daddy exclaimed as Robert laughed...

"What's so funny Daddy?" Mommy asked...

"That's the same thing I said to your mother..." Robert laughed...

"Good – now do you want Tiramisu or Cannoli Dip with Fresh Fruit and Crushed Cannoli Shells?" Bri asked...

"I want the Cannoli Dip with Fresh Fruit and Crushed Cannoli Shells!" Mommy exclaimed...

"Okay!" I'll get this booked asap! You can both go now!"

"Okay Mommy – Bye!" Mommy laughed as they left and Bri closed the door behind them...

"I gotta go..." Daddy said as he kissed Mommy... "I'll talk to you later..."

"Okay..." Mommy sighed...

"Don't worry – after we get married I won't leave you again..."

"You promise?"

"Promise..."

"Hi..." Daddy sighed...

"What's wrong?" Ryan asked...

"Nothing..."

"Come here..." Ryan commanded...

"Yes Dad?"

"What happened between the time you left here and the time you left there?"

"I went over there to see where she wanted to get married..."

"You didn't have any input?"

"I don't care where we get married – I just want her to be happy..."

Did she pick a place?"

"Yea..."

"What's wrong – you don't like it?"

"She picked the Stonecroft Country Inn..."

"Oh wow – that's nice!" Joshy said as she came downstairs..."

"You've seen it Joshy?" Ryan asked...

"Yea – my co-worker got married there last year – you'll love it – it's really romantic..."

"I hope so..." Daddy sighed...

"Ryan – what's wrong?" Joshy asked...

"She wants to go to Hawaii for our honeymoon..." Daddy sighed...

"What's wrong with that?" Joshy asked...

"We can't afford Hawaii..." Daddy sighed...

"Son – we gotchu..." Ryan said...

"Dad – I can't ask you to do that – you're already paying for me to go to Harvard..."

"Ryan – the bulk of your tuition is covered by your scholarship – c'mon – let's go in your room – I have something to show you..." Joshy said as Daddy followed her into his room...

"Turn on your computer..." Ryan said...

"Okay..." Daddy sighed...

"Type in unforgatablehoneymoons.com..." Joshy said...

"Oh wow..." Daddy exclaimed as he looked at the honeymoon packages...

"See the honeymoon packages in Hawaii?" Ryan asked... "Look at the packages, pick the one you want, and we'll take care of it..."

"Mom... Dad..." Daddy whispered as he started crying... "I love you so much..."

"We love you too – now hurry up and pick out the package you want so we can book it..." Joshy said...

"Okay..." Daddy said as he looked at the packages...

"This one..." Daddy said as he pointed at the computer...

"Almost All Inclusive Oahu Honeymoon at Hyatt Regency Waikiki Beach... that's nice!" Joshy exclaimed...

"We have access to the Regency Club, we can walk to the beach, we have a private lanai, there's a torch-lighting ceremony on Kuhio Beach at sunset, and if we stay 5 nights, we get one free..."

"Okay – when do you wanna leave?" Joshy asked...

"Wednesday, June 30th..."

"Okay – I'll go book this right now..." Joshy said...

"What if you can't get the hotel?" Daddy asked...

"You let me worry about that..." Joshy said as she left the room. Joshy wasn't gone for long... "You're all set..." she said as she came back into the room... "I went to another site..." she beamed...

"Mom... Dad... Thank you..."

"You're welcome..." Joshy said...

"I'll tell Cyn after we get married..."

"That's a great idea..." Ryan said...

Chapter TWENTY-FOUR

“Hi Ally! Hi Ms. Alice!” Mommy exclaimed as they got in the car…

“Hi Cyn – good morning Ms. Bri – where are we going?” Ally asked...

“We’re going to David’s Bridal in Orange…” Alice answered...

“Oh wow – I’ve never been there…” Ally said...

“Me either Mommy said... did you go to David’s Bridal when you got married Mommy?”

“Yes Cyn…” Bri answered as she drove…

“Hi Joshy...” Bri said as she got in the car...

“Good morning everybody...” Joshy said...

“Good morning...” they all said in unison...

“After we pick up Regina, we’ll head straight there...” Bri said...

"Damn – I could sure use a cup of coffee…" Joshy said...

"When we get to David's Bridal, there's a Subway across the street and a gas station – we can stop in there for coffee if you want…" Bri said…

"Thank you Bri – I just ain't right without my coffee…"

"I know what you mean..." Bri said as they pulled up in front of Regina's house Cyn opened the car door...

"Good morning everyone!" Regina said as she got in the car...

"Good morning!" everyone said in unison...

"Are we going to get dresses or are we going to get our hair, nails, and feet done?"

"We're going to David's Bridal..." Bri answered...

"Can we stop for coffee?" Regina asked...

"We're stopping for coffee..." Joshy laughed...

"Mommy – look! We're here! I'm so excited!" Mommy squealed...

"Le'me park the car Cyn…" Bri laughed…

"Oh good I can get my coffee..." Regina said...

"We can go for coffee if you want – but I don't know if they'll let you inside with it…" Bri said...

"I'll get a small coffee…" Joshy said...

"Me too..." Regina said...

"I thought we were going to Subway?" Joshy asked…

"The coffee is always better at gas stations…" Bri answered…

"Okay – I'll be quick…" Regina said as she made her coffee…"

"Let me pay for this and we can be on our way…" Joshy said…

"I already took care of it…" Bri said…

"Thank you…"

"You're welcome – c'mon – Cyn's getting ansy…" Bri said as Cyn and Ally got out the car, ran across the street and beat them to the entrance…

"Welcome to David's Bridal – may I help you?"

"She's getting married on Monday, June 28th…" Bri answered…

"Will you be needing dresses as well?"

"Yes we will…" Bri answered…

"Which one of you is the Mother of the Bride?"

"I am…" Bri beamed…"

"Will you be wearing a white dress?"

"Yes she will!" Bri answered before Mommy could say anything…

"About what size are you?" the lady asked Mommy...

"I'm a size 8…"

"Dresses in your size are in the back to the right – dressed for you ladies are to the left – my name is Lisa – take your time – when you're ready I'll come assist you…"

"Thank you Lisa…" Bri said as she took Mommy's hand "Let's go ladies – somebody's getting married!" Bri exclaimed as she smiled…

"Oh my God – there's too many dresses…" Mommy laughed…

"I'll help you..." Ally said...

"Did you look at the website?' Joshy asked…

"Yes – but there's so many!"

"Okay – we know you want a white dress – right?" Ally asked...

"Yes!"

"Okay – do you want a dress that comes out like Cinderella or do you want a dress that shows your curves?"

"I wanna show off my curves…"

"Okay – they have a Mermaid Trumpet and they have Sheath – the Mermaid comes out at the bottom and the Sheath goes straight down – I think you should go with the Mermaid because it will accentuate your curves – I'll show you – this is a Mermaid Trumpet style – this is a Sheath style – which one do you like?"

"Mommy – help me… please…" Mommy laughed...

"Take one of each – try them both on – see which one you like the best…" Bri said…

"That's a good idea Mommy – thank you…" Mommy said as she started looking at the dresses… "I like this one!" Mommy yelled as she picked up the Sweetheart Trumpet Wedding Dress with Beads Sash…

"It's beautiful…" Bri said…

"It is beautiful…" Joshy said…

"I'll help you try it on..." Ally said...

"Okay – we'll be right back…"

"Regina?"

"Yes Ally?"

"I need help..." Ally laughed...

"C'mon – we'll go look at some dresses..." Regina said. Bri waited outside for a few moments, Mommy came out wearing the wedding dress, stood in front of the mirror… and started crying…

"What's wrong Baby? You don't like it?" Bri asked...

"Oh my God… this is my dress…"

"Yes it is…" Bri agreed…

"Can I get it?"

"Of course…" Bri said…

"Ryan's going to fall in love with you all over again…" Joshy said…

"Yes he is... C'mon – let's get this dress off…" Bri said as Lisa came over…

"How's it going?"

"She found her dress…" Bri said…

"Wonderful! Do you want the veil, the necklace, and the pearl bracelets as well?"

"Can I get them Mommy... please?"

"Of course..."

"Oh Mommy – thank you, thank you, thank you!" Mommy yelled as she jumped up and down hugging Bri...

"You're welcome..." Bri laughed...

"What size shoes do you wear?" Lisa asked...

"I wear a size 6..."

"Okay – here's our catalog of wedding shoes – personally I think you should go with the High-Heeled Sandals with Crystal Flower Strap by Vera Wang – they'll bring out the crystal in your dress and show off your pedicure..."

"I love them!"

"Yes Cyn – you can have them..." Bri laughed...

"Okay – now you'll definitely want to be comfortable at the reception – here's our catalog of wedges and flats..."

"I want these!" Cyn yelled as she pointed at the Crystal-Topped Wedge Sandals with Ankle Strap...

"Nice choice!" I'll put everything up front with your name on it – what's your name?"

"Cynthia..."

"Okay Cynthia..." Lisa said as she took everything up front...

"Are you getting a dress as well?" Lisa asked...

"Yes I am – and so is Joshy..." Bri answered...

"Which one of you is the mother of the Bride?" Lisa asked...

"I'm the mother of the Bride – Joshy is the mother of the Groom – Regina is the mother of the Best Man – and Alice is the mother of the Best Friend..."

"Oh okay – let's see what we have..." Lisa said as they followed Lisa to look at dresses...

"Found it!" Bri said as she pulled a Sequin Lace Mermaid Dress with Illusion Detail off the rack...

"Found it!" Joshy said as she pulled a Sequin Damask Pattern Sheath Dress with Sash off the rack...

"Found it!" Alice said as she pulled a Short Sleeve Sequin Lace and Mikado Midi Dress off the rack...

"Found it!" Regina said as she pulled a Jersey Sheath Gown with Sequin Capelet off the rack...

"Oooohhh! Le'me see!" Mommy exclaimed when she saw the dresses...

"Found it!" Ally said as she came over holding a Glitter Accent Drape Sleeve Stretch Sheath Dress...

"Ally! I love it!" Mommy exclaimed...

"I see you're all feeling blue..." Lisa laughed...

"I guess we are..." Bri laughed...

"Mommy – go try on the dress – I wanna see!" Mommy exclaimed...

"Okay – c'mon Ally – c'mon ladies – let's go try on our dresses..." Bri said as they all went into the large dressing room...

"Everything okay in there ladies?" Lisa asked…

"Yes – we'll be right out…" Bri said as they came out…

"Mommy... you look so pretty!" Mommy exclaimed...

"Thank you Cyn – but I'll never be as pretty as the Bride..." Bri said...

"Oh my God – Ally!" Mommy exclaimed...

"You like it?" Ally asked...

"I sure do!" Alice exclaimed!

"Thank you Mommy..." Ally said...

"We all look good..." Regina said as she showed her leg peeking from under her dress...

"Aww shit... git it Mother!" Bri said as everyone laughed...

"I guess you'll be taking these..." Lisa said...

"Yes we will..." Bri acknowledged...

"Okay Ladies – I know you want comfortable shoes…" Lisa laughed as she showed Bri the catalog…

"I want these right here…" she said as she pointed to the Pink Paradox Strappy Shimmer T-Strap Mules…

"What size?"

"Size 8…"

"Okay – how about you?" Lisa asked as she showed the catalog to Joshy……

"I'll take those too..." Joshy said... "Size 8..."

"I'll take those too..." Ally said... "Size 6..."

"I'll take these right here…" Alice said as she pointed to the Wendie Glitter Peep Toe Wedge…

"And what size do you need?"

"Size 6 – cause – unlike somebody else – my feet ain't swollen..." Alice laughed...

"Oh so you wanna throw shade?" Regina laughed...

"I'ma remember that shit next time you want a cup of coffee…" Bri laughed…

"I'll take those too..." Regina said... "Size 8..."

"Okay Ladies… now that you've picked out your dresses and your accessories – it's time to let the bride prepare for her wedding night…" Lisa said as we walked to the front of the store…

"Oh wow – I can't wait!" Mommy yelled…

"Here's a sample of everything we have in the glass cases – take your time – if you see something you like – let me know and I'll go get it…" Lisa said as she walked away to help another customer…

"I need something for your wedding night too…" Bri laughed…

"Why Mommy – it's not your night…"

"I'm still a woman – I can look sexy – it might be just for me – but I can still look sexy..." Bri laughed..."

"I like almost everything in here Mommy..." Mommy said as she looked through the cases...

"Take your time – pick what you want – we have all afternoon..." Bri said... "Oh – Cyn – get this!" Bri exclaimed as she pointed to a sleep shirt that said: I Woke Up Like This #Married...

"Okay!" Mommy squealed...

"Cyn – you need this Wedding Dress Bag..." Joshy said...

"Okay..."

"Get this All Over Beaded Vintage Inspired Garter – you need to wear that on your wedding day under your dress..." Bri said...

"Nobody's gonna see it..." Mommy said...

"Honey – when you have your reception – Ryan will sit you in the chair, lift up your dress, and take off the garter with his teeth..." Bri said...

"Oh my God – he will?"

"Yes Cyn – it's tradition..." Joshy said...

"How's everything going?" Lisa asked as she came over...

"Everything's fine – we're ready..." Bri said

"Your father was in here the other day..." Lisa said...

"He was?" Mommy asked...

"Yes... he already has an account with us..."

"Oh yea – that was opened when we were married..." Bri said...

"I'll get everything ready – Bri – go get your car and bring it to the front – I want to get everything in the car before the guys get here..."

"The guys?" Bri asked...

"Yes – your husband is on his way – and we don't want Cyn's fiancée to see anything before their wedding..."

"Oh wow – that's great – everyone can get taken care of here – I didn't know you could take care of the guys – I thought David's Bridal was just for Ladies!" Ally laughed...

"Yes – now go get your car – and I'll make sure everything's ready..." Lisa said as she hurried off...

"Cyn – I need a minute to sit down – can you go get the car for me?" Bri asked as she handed Mommy the keys...

"Sure!" Mommy squealed as she took the keys and ran to get the car...

"The car's outside Mommy..." Mommy said as she handed the keys to Bri...

"Thank you for calling David's Bridal – this is Lisa... Yes Mr. Lawrence – we'll see you soon..." Lisa said as she hung up...

"C'mon –let's get outta here!" Bri exclaimed as Lisa loaded everything into the car and they headed towards Milford Mall...

"They gone?" Ryan asked as he came inside with Daddy…

"They're gone…" Robert answered…

"How much time we got?"

"Hmmm… Let's see… my wife, my daughter, her mother… and a Black American Express card…"

"Shit – we good for the rest of the day!" Ryan said as Ryan, Daddy, and Robert laughed…

"Robert – we good?" Ronald asked as he came in with Chip…

"We good - c'mon in – we're in the living room!" Robert answered…

"Hey Ryans…" Ronald said when he saw them…

"Hey Ronald…" Ryan said…

"Hi Mr. Ronald..." Daddy said...

"Hi everybody..." Chip said...

"Who we waiting for?" Ronald asked…

"Phillip… " Robert answered…

"Where's everybody at?" Phillip asked...

"We're in the living room!" Robert yelled…

"Hey!" Phillip said as he came into the living room…

"Hey Phillip…" everyone said in unison...

"Who's driving?" Phillip asked…

"Nobody…" Robert answered…

"Nobody?" Phillip asked…

"We're drinking…" Robert answered…

"Oh… okay!" Phillip laughed… Speaking of drinking – where we goin'?"

"You'll find out when we get there – but first – we need to get there – I ordered a car for us – he should be outside now…" Robert said as he went to the door… "It's here – let's go…" Robert said as he opened the door and they all went outside and got in the limousine. Robert smiled to himself watching the way Chip was in awe…

"Where we goin' first?" Chip asked…

"We're going to David's Bridal..." Robert answered…

"Isn't that for Women?" Daddy asked...

"It's for Men too…" Robert answered…

"Hmmm... okay... I need some coffee…" Phillip said…

"I need some Henney!" Ronald said as everyone laughed…

"We need to drink coffee before we drink anything else..." Robert said... "Unless you don't drink coffee – then you need milk – but we're all men here – right?"

"Right!" they answered in unison....

"Okay – Mike – pull into the Dunkin Donuts on the left..."

"Yes Mr. Lawrence..." Mike answered as he pulled into the parking lot... "Would you like to go through the drive through or shall I park?"

"Let's go through the drive through..."

"Yes Mr. Lawrence..." Mike said as he drove the limousine around to the drive through..."

"Welcome to Dunkin Donuts – may I take your order?"

"Yes Maam – hold on one moment – Mr. Lawrence - what would you like?" Mike asked...

"We'll have six medium coffees – hazelnut swirl – with cream..."

"Coming right up Mr. Lawrence..." Mike said as he repeated their order to the cashier...

"Here you are..." The cashier said as she passed the coffees to Mike...

"Thank ya Maam..." Mike said as he took the coffees and passed them back to everyone..."Here's the credit card..." Mike said...

"Okay – I'll be right back..." the cashier said as she went to pay for the order. When she was done she came back to the car and handed it to Mike...

"Okay – thank ya Maam... have a good day..." Mike said as he closed up the windows and drove off... "Thanks for the coffee Mr. Lawrence..."

"You're welcome Mike..."

"Mr. Lawrence – we're here – would you like for me to wait in the parking lot for you?"

"Yes Mike..." Robert answered...

"Okay – do you mind if I park, go get some breakfast – and come right back?"

"That's fine Mike..."

"Okay – thank you Mr. Lawrence – I'll let you out..." he said as he got out and opened the door for them..."

"You ready Ryan? His father asked him...

"Yea... I think so..."

"Don't be nervous – it's just the first day of the rest of your life..." Ryan said......

"Exactly – pop ups at the job – angry texts when you don't respond in two seconds – mood swings..." Robert laughed...

"Yo – wait – the best is when she expects you to know why she mad talkin' 'bout you know what the fuck you did!" Ronald laughed...

"Oh my God – yes!" Phillip said as they all laughed...

"Ummm... y'all are not helping..." Daddy laughed as they all went inside...

"Welcome to David's Bridal – my name is Lisa – I'll be taking care of you this afternoon – may I have your name please?"

"Mr. Lawrence..."

"Mr. Lawrence – welcome back – it'll be my pleasure to take care of your wedding needs – who's the lucky groom?"

"My future son-in-law – Ryan Davis..." Robert answered as he brought Daddy up to the front...

"Oh my – I'm going to love this..." Lisa said as she ran her hands down Daddy's shoulders and across his chest...

"I'ma need you to slow down Lisa...." Daddy said...

"Oh my goodness – I'm sorry – I didn't mean to offend you – I was just taking a quick measurement – everyone else uses measuring tape but I'm usually pretty accurate by feeling my way around..." she laughed...

"Shit – you ever have any wives run up on you when you're feeling on their husbands?" Ryan asked...

"A few – but I don't take it personal..."

"So... you need to feel your way around me?" Robert laughed...

"Yes... if you're buying a suit..."

"Hmmm... okay..."

"C'mon guys – let's get you in and out..." she said as she took them in the back to the men's section... "We have complete packages starting at $99.00..." she said as they started looking at suits... "We have Black by Vera Wang and Joseph Abound – personally I think Joseph Abound is the right choice for you…"

"Why?" Daddy asked…

"Black men are built different – you have broad chests and shoulders – white men are more straight up and down with small, round butts…"

"Okay!" Ronald laughed…

"When you've been feeling men as long as I have – you get to know all the shapes and sizes…" Lisa laughed…

"What colors do you have?" Phillip asked…

"We have black, gray, and navy…"

"I'd like navy…" Daddy said…

"Okay – I'll be back with the suit and the accessories – what size shoe do you wear?"

"I'm a 9..."

"Okay – I'll be right back…"

"Nice choice…" Robert said…

"Thanks Mr. Robert…"

"Here you are…" Lisa said as she came back with everything…"

"Hmmm… a pink tie…" Daddy said…

"Try it on – it looks great with the navy – and it'll also go great with your complexion…"

"Thank you – I'll be right back…" Daddy said as he went into the dressing room…

"Oh wow…" Ryan said when Daddy came out and stood in front of the mirror…

"You look good Ryan..." Robert said…

"That's the one…" Ronald said…

"Okay Ryan!" Phillip said…

"You look great!" Lisa said...

"I'll take everything..." Daddy said...

"Okay – I'll bring these items up front and I'll be right back..." she said as she took the items to the front...

"So what color should we get?" Ryan asked...

"I like the dark gray..." Ronald said...

"So do I..." Phillip said...

"I like the dark gray too..." Robert said...

"I like the black one..." Chip said...

"Have you all decided what you'd like?" Lisa asked...

"I'd like the Navy suit..." Ryan said as he went over to Lisa...

"Mr. Lawrence – I don't need to feel you up – we have your measurements from your wedding..." she laughed...

"You came to David's Bridal for your wedding?" Phillip asked...

"Yes..."

"Where were you married?"

"In Vegas..."

"Oh nice! They have a David's Bridal in Vegas?"

"Yes they do..."

"Mr. Lawrence – would you like all the accessories?"

"Yes Lisa..."

"How 'bout the tie?"

"I'll take it..."

"That Monaco Quartz will look great on you – I'll be right back..." she said as she went to get the suit and accessories, and then she took them up front... "I took everything up front – is that alright?"

"That's fine..."

"Okay then – who am I feeling up next?" Lisa asked as she put up her hands...

"Me..." Phillip laughed as he walked over to her and she felt his shoulders, his chest, and put her arms around his waist...

"Hmmm... I got it – what size shoes?"

"I'm a 9..."

"Okay – I'll be back in a sec..." Lisa came right back and handed everything to Phillip...

"Thank you Lisa..." Phillip said as he sat down...

"You're welcome – aren't you going to try it on?"

"I'ma wait for them..."

"Okay – who's next?" Lisa said as she put up her hands...

"Me..." Ronald said as he went over to Lisa and she felt his shoulders, his chest, and hugged him...

"Ummm... okay..." Ronald laughed...

"I'm sorry – you're not as tall as Phillip..." she laughed...

"Oh – so you hug the short men..." Ronald laughed...

"Yes – if they let me – hugging them gives me a more accurate measurement..."

"Okay – last but not least – come here..." she said as she went over to Chip, felt his shoulders, his chest, and hugged him... "Hmmm... - you're both just about the same – If I didn't know any better I'd say you were brothers..." she said as she went to the back..."

"She's good..." Robert laughed...

"I wonder if she's married..." Phillip said...

"I sure wouldn't want my wife feeling on men all day..." Ronald said...

"Wouldn't bother me one bit..." Ryan said...

"Yea right!" Robert laughed...

"I'm serious..." Ryan said...

"Seriously?" Phillip asked...

"Phillip..." Ryan said as he went over to Phillip and put his arm around him... "The only dick my wife wants... is mine..."

"I know that's right!" Robert said as they high-fived...

"Okay guys – here ya go..." Lisa said as she handed Ronald and Chip the suits and accessories...

"Thank you Lisa..." they said in unison...

"You're welcome – now go try those on – I wanna see!"

"Okay, okay..." Daddy laughed as they went to try on everything...

"Oh my God – I need a phone – gimmie a phone..." Lisa exclaimed... as Daddy and Ryan came out...

"Here – take mine..." Ryan said...

"Okay guys – he's your first picture – get in there..."

"Wait – Ronald and Chip aren't wearing their clothes..." Daddy said...

"Doesn't matter..." Lisa said as she took the picture... "Here Ryan..." she said as she handed him the phone... "Okay guys – go change so I can get you outta here..." she said as Robert waited with Lisa for them to come out... "Okay – I'll get these things up front... come with me..." she said as they followed her up front... "Okay – we have some other accessories here in the glass case – if you see anything you like, just let me know..." she said as she went to put everything in bags...

"I like this Kimono Robe..." Daddy said...

"I like it too..." Ryan said...

"Get it..." Robert said...

"Okay..." Daddy said... "But I need you to get these cuff links..." Daddy said as he pointed to the cuff links...

"Aww... that's what's up..." Phillip said...

"Best Dad... nice..." Ronald said...

"Ryan... that isn't necessary..." Robert said...

"I'ma tell you like you told me – get it..." Daddy said as they all laughed...

"Fine – I'll get it – thank you Ryan..."

"You're welcome... Dad..."

"I love y'all..." Phillip said..."

"Okay – everybody's getting this money clip!" Chip exclaimed...

"Okay!" they all said in unison...

"And everybody needs to have it in their pocket on Ryan's wedding Day..."

"Okay!" they all said in unison again...

"Okay – you guys wanna go out for a bit and come back?" Lisa asked...

"Okay – we'll come back..." Robert answered... "C'mon guys – let's get outta here for a bit..." Robert said as he went out and they followed him to the limousine...

"Hey guys – how'd everything go?" Mike asked...

"Everything's fine Mike..." Robert answered as they got in the limousine...

"You headed back home?"

"Not yet..."

"Where shall I take you next?"

"Andinis..."

"Okay Mr. Lawrence – Andinis it is..."Mike said as they drove off towards the restaurant...

"What kind of restaurant is Andinis?" Ryan asked…

"It's Italian…"

"Nice…" Ryan said…

"It is – I've been there myself…" Mike said…

"Oh…."

"We're here – I'll let you out…" Mike said as he got out and opened the door for them…

"Thank you Mike – we'll see you in about an hour…" Robert said as they went into the restaurant…

"Welcome to Andinis – nice to see you again Mr. Lawrence – right this way…" the hostess said as she took them to the table… "The waitress will be here to take your orders – we have some new items on the menu…" the hostess said…

"Hello Mr. Lawrence – nice to see you again…" Carmen said as she came over to the table… "May I start you off with some appetizers?"

"Yes – we'll have Risotto Balls, Veal Meatballs, Rabe & Sausage, Fried Calamari – and Samuel Adams for everybody…"

"Okay – I'll be back with your drinks and appetizers…" she said as she went to place the order…

"This is my first time here…" Chip said…

"You'll like it…" Robert said as Carmen came back with their beers and put them on the table…

"To Ryan…" Robert said as he raised his glass…

"To Ryan…" they all said in unison…

"I'm proud to have you as my son-in-law…" Robert said...

"Thanks Dad…" Daddy said and then they all took a sip…

"Here are your appetizers…" Carmen said as she placed them on the table… "Can I get you refills?"

"Yes – please…" Robert said…

"Coming right up…" Carmen said as she took their glasses and then went to get them refills…

"Eat! Eat!" Robert said as everyone started eating…

"Here's your drinks…" Carmen said as she put their beers on the table… "Are you guys ready to order?"

"We'll have the NY Strip Steak…" Robert answered…

"Regular or Cesar?"

"Regular…"

"Okay – pasta or baked potato?"

"Baked potato…"

"How would you like your steak?"

"Medium well…"

"Does that work for everybody?"

"I'd like well done…" Ryan said…

"Anyone else?"

"I'd like well done..." Daddy said...

"Well done for us too…" Ronald said…

"Yea – well done…" Phillip and Chip agreed…

"Okay – 1 medium well, 5 well-done – I'll be back…" Carmen said as she walked away…

"I can't wait for this to be over…" Daddy sighed...

"Over?" Robert asked…

"I just want us to be married…"

"Aww… you love her…" Chip said…

"Yea…"

"She loves you too…" Ronald said…

"I know…"

"We were just like that in the beginning..." Phillip said...

"Me 'n Bri are still like that..." Robert said...

"My wife and I are all over each other..." Ryan said...

"Here's your steaks – 1 medium well – 5 well done – backed potatoes, and salads – can I get you anything else?" Carmen asked...

"Yea – A1!" Daddy answered...

"I'll be back..." Carmen said...

"Oh damn!" Ryan said as he tasted his steak...

"Good – right?" Robert asked...

"Hell yea!" Ryan smacked...

"Can your wife cook steak?" Ronald asked...

"Oh yea – but this right here – she might have a lil' competition..." Ryan laughed...

"Bri's like her father – she cooked for me the first night I invited her to my place - I walked in from work and she had dinner ready for me..." Robert sighed...

"Joshy gets it in – I move out her way – and stay out her way..." Ryan laughed...

"Here's your A1..." Carmen said as she placed the bottle on the table... "If you need anything else – I'll be over there..." she said as she walked away and they continued...

"My wife gets down... and so do I..." Ronald said......

"I do the cooking in my house..." Phillip said...

"Your wife can't cook?" Ronald asked...

"I won't let her..."

"Why?"

"I love cooking for her..."

"Aww..." Chip said...

"Well..." Robert said as he rubbed his stomach... "I guess we better go get our things before they think we forgot..."

"Oh my God..." Ronald laughed as he got up and stretched... "I'm so full – my wife's gonna be mad if I can't eat dinner..."

"No she won't – you're with me – remember?" Robert laughed...

"Oh yea – I'm good – she likes you..." Ronald laughed as they all got up from the table...

"I'll meet you guys outside..." Robert said as he went to pay the check...

"Thank you Mr. Lawrence – always a pleasure..." Carmen said...

"You're welcome – I'll see you again..." Robert said as he left the restaurant and went to get in the limousine...

"Back to David's Bridal?" Mike asked...

"Yes Mike..."

"Okay Mr. Lawrence..." Mike said as they drove off...

"Mr. Lawrence – I was just getting ready to call you..." Lisa said as they walked in...

"Is everything ready?" Robert asked...

"Yes – let me show you how the engraved money clips came out..." she said as she took the money clips out to show them...

"Oh yes – this is exactly what I wanted..." Robert said...

"Nice... thanks Dad..." Daddy said. Ryan, Ronald, Chip, and Phillip nodded in approval...

"Everything's ready for you to take to the car – if you have any problems or you need anything – you can call me directly..."

"Thank you Lisa..." Robert said...

"You're welcome Mr. Lawrence – have a great day – and congratulations Ryan..." she said as she went to help another customer...

"What a great day..." Daddy said as they got in the limousine...

"Yes it was..." Ryan agreed...

"Mike – we're going home..." Robert said...

"Okay Mr. Lawrence..." Mike said as he drove off. When they got to the house, Mike opened the door, Robert got out, and then he took out his bags...

"Guys – we're gonna go in the library – leave your things in the car..."

"Okay..." they said in unison as they followed Robert into the house and into the library...

"Guys - you know what to do – I'll be right back..." Robert said as he took his bags upstairs. Daddy got five glasses and Ryan got the bottle of

Hennessey and poured them all drinks... "Bri? Bri - are you in here?" Robert asked. When he didn't get an answer he was relieved and headed back to the library... "Let's do this!" Robert said as they spent the rest of the afternoon drinking, laughing, and talking...

Chapter TWENTY-SEVEN

"Ladies – let's go!" Bri said…

"I'm coming!" Mommy squealed as she came into the dressing room…

"Cyn – I need you to take these bags to your room and come right back – we need to get your hair done and get you ready for your husband…"

"Okay!" she squealed as she grabbed the bags and ran downstairs to their room. When she came out, she ran right into Daddy…

"Hey…" Daddy said as he pulled her into a kiss…

"Hey…" Mommy breathed…

"We're getting married…"

"I know…"

"Cyn – let's go!" Bri yelled…

"I'm coming!" Mommy yelled as she flew upstairs…

"Aiight guys – let's go!" Robert said…

"Where we goin'?" Daddy asked…

"In the dressing room guys…" Scott's assistant said as he stuck his head out the room…

"You ready Ryan?" Robert asked as they all went into the room…

"Hell yea!"

"Me too…" Ryan said as he pulled Daddy into a hug…

"Dad…" Daddy said as he started crying…

"Don't start that shit!" Ronald laughed…

"I was a nervous wreck on my wedding day…" Phillip said…

"We all were…" Ryan said…

"I cried right along with Bri…" Robert said…

"Oh my God… look at my Baby…" Bri whispered as she started to cry…

"Mommy… please don't cry…" Mommy said as she started crying…

"I love you so much…" Bri said as they hugged each other…

"I love you too Mommy…" Mommy cried…

"Aiight – break it up – Bri – get dressed - Cyn – get your garter belt on – matter fact – Bri - – put this on her thigh…" Jodie said…

"Yes Maam…" Bri laughed…

"Ally – you look pretty!" Mommy exclaimed…

"Cyn…" Ally said as they started hugging each other…

"I love you…" Mommy said…

"I love you too…"

"Is this where we get ready?" Joshy asked as she came inside…

"Yes – c'mon in…" Bri said as Regina and Alice came into the dressing room…

"You look good Ryan…" Chip said…

"Thanks – you look good too…"

"Look at my son!" Ryan said…

"You lookin' sharp Ryan!" Robert said…

"Ahem!" Ronald interrupted…

"Aww shit!" Phillip said…

"Okay Ronald – I see you!" Ryan said…

"We ready?" Robert asked…

"We ready!" they all said in unison…

"Okay – let's go!" Robert said as they all went downstairs…

Chapter Twenty-Eight

The videographer and photographer were ready. Mommy's father walked her down the aisle and Mommy burst into tears when she saw Daddy and Reverend Woody. Mommy looked out and everyone was crying. Daddy's father stood beside Daddy, and Mommy's father stood beside Mommy. After everyone gathered themselves and wiped away their make-up along with their tears, the wedding continued...

"Beloved... we are gathered here this afternoon to join Cynthia Lawrence, Ryan Davis, and their Christmas Miracle in marriage. You have both come before me, expressed your desire to become husband and wife. Do you have rings?"

"Yes – we have rings..." Ryan said as he took two ring boxes out his pocket...

"Okay – take the rings out the boxes – Cyn – you take his ring – Ryan – you take her ring…"

"Okay…" Mommy and Daddy said in unison as Mommy took Daddy's ring and Daddy took Mommy's ring...

"Who gives this woman to be married? Reverend Woody asked…

"I do…" Robert answered…

"Okay – Ryan – do you have anything you want to say to Cyn?"

"Yes I do…" Daddy answered as he took Mommy's hands...

"Cyn, when I first met you, I was intimidated by you. You were so full of confidence and swag I didn't think I stood a chance. Thank you for taking a chance on me and making me the luckiest man in the world. I promise to love you more than I do now – if that's possible – I promise to love our Christmas Miracle, and I promise to be the best and only husband you'll ever have..."

"Okay – Cyn – do you have anything you want to say to Ryan?"

"Yes I do…" Mommy answered as she took Daddy's hands...

"Ryan, when I first saw you, I literally said to Ally – Oh God – here he comes..." Mommy said as everyone laughed. When you introduced yourself to me, as shy as you were, I was impressed with you. You were so sweet and genuine, I couldn't say no. Thank you for loving me enough to ask me to be your wife. I promise to love you more than I do now, I promise to love our Christmas Miracle, and I promise to be the best and only wife you'll ever have..."

"Okay – Ryan, Cyn – do you have anything you want to say to your Christmas Miracle?"

"Yes we do..." Mommy and Daddy answered in unison as Daddy took Mommy's hands, placed their hands on Mommy's stomach and then they married me...

"Our Christmas Miracle, Mommy and Daddy are so happy that you're here. When the doctor told us it was a miracle Mommy was pregnant, we knew you were mean to be. We promise to love you more than we do now, we promise to be the best parents we can be, and we promise to help you become the best person you can be..."

"Aww... I love you Mommy... I love you Daddy..." I was so happy I started releasing endorphins and serotonin, and I cried along with Mommy and Daddy as Reverend Wood spoke...

"Ryan – put the ring on Cyn's finger and repeat after me..." Reverend Woody said...

"Okay – I'm ready..." Daddy said...

"Cyn – I take you as my wife, with your faults and your strengths, as I offer myself to you with my faults and my strengths..." Daddy repeated after Reverend Woody and then she continued... "I will help you when you need help and turn to you when I need help. Today - I choose to spend the rest of my life with you..." Mommy started crying as Ryan repeated the vows to her. When he was finished, Daddy took Mommy's face in his hands and kissed her...

"Cyn – put the ring on Ryan's finger and repeat after me..."

"Okay – I'm ready..." Mommy said...

"Ryan - I take you as my husband, with your faults and your strengths, as I offer myself to you with my faults and my strengths. I will help you when you need help and turn to you when I need help. Today – I choose to spend the rest of my life with you..." Daddy cried as Mommy repeated the vows to him. When she was finished, Mommy took Daddy's face in her hands and kissed him...

"Ryan, Cyn, you have come before God, your parents, and your friends to pledge your love and commitment to each other and your

Christmas Miracle. By the power invested in me by God and to me by the State of Connecticut, I now pronounce you husband and wife..." Mommy and Daddy were kissing before she could tell Daddy to kiss his bride so she laughed and then she said... "It's my pleasure to introduce Mr. & Mrs. Ryan Davis, and Christmas Miracle Davis..."

"I have a surprise for you..." Daddy whispered to Mommy...

"I have a surprise for you too..." Mommy whispered to Daddy...

"Okay – we need everyone outside..." the videographer said as he motioned for the photographer and everyone else to follow him outside. After everyone got outside the videographer set up the camcorder and the photographer took pictures of Mommy and Daddy by themselves and then they took group pictures... "Okay – we'll get some pictures in the dining room while you're eating..." the photographer said as he motioned for everyone to go into the dining room...

"Ryan…" Mommy whispered as she heard All of My Love playing…

"I love you Mrs. Davis…" Daddy said as he pulled Mommy into his arms and they danced…

"I love you too Mr. Davis..." Mommy whispered in his ear..."

"I can't wait to get you upstairs..."

"Me either..."

"I'm gonna put it on you something fierce..."

"I know..." Mommy breathed. The song was over and they stood in the middle of the floor holding each other and kissing as everyone applauded...

"I love you..." Daddy breathed as he kissed Mommy...

"I love you too..." Mommy breathed. Daddy pulled Mommy into another kiss and held her as everyone applauded again. Robert started tapping his champagne glass and everyone else did the same as they continued kissing...

"Come with me Mrs. Davis..." Daddy said as he took Mommy's hand and led her to the head of the table, pulled out the chair, waited for her to sit down, and then he sat down beside her. Ryan sat next to Daddy, Bri sat next to Mommy, Alice sat next to Bri, Ally sat next to Alice, Regina sat next to Ally, and Phillip sat next to Chip.

A bottle of Prosecco was sitting in the middle of the table and the glasses were already filled. Robert stood up and started crying. Daddy stood up beside him and started crying too...

"Ryan..." was all my Robert was able to get out. Daddy pulled Robert into a hug and cried with him, Ryan stood up, and then Daddy pulled Ryan into a hug and cried with him... "Ryan... you respected me enough to ask me for my blessing before you proposed to my daughter – and in that moment – I saw the man my daughter fell in love with – and I'm so proud to call you my son-in-law..."

"Aww..." Daddy said as he started crying...

"I love you son..." Ryan said as he hugged Daddy and cried along with everybody else...

"Cyn..." Robert said as he extended his hand to help Mommy stand beside him...

"Yes Daddy?" Mommy whispered as tears streamed down her face...

"I love you..." he said as he took Mommy's face in his hands and wiped her tears...

"I love you too Daddy..."

"Aww..." everyone said in unison...

"Cyn..." Bri said as she stood up... "My beautiful baby girl..." she said as she teared up... "I love you..."

"I love you too Mommy..."

"I'm so proud of the woman you've become... and as much as I'd like to take all the credit... I can't... Ryan... Thank you for loving my daughter..."

"Aww..." everyone said in unison...

"Cyn..." Ryan said as he stood up... "My son couldn't have chosen better than you..."

"Aww..." everyone said in unison...

"Cyn..." Ally said a she stood up...

"Yes Ally?" Mommy said as Ally ran to Mommy and they hugged each other and cried...

"Aww..." everyone said in unison...

"Ryan..." Chip said as he stood up...

"I'm really happy for you both..."

"Thanks Chip..." Daddy said...

"Okay – everyone raise your glass!" Robert said... "To Mr. & Mrs. Davis!" Robert said as he took a sip of champagne...

"To Mr. & Mrs. Davis!" everyone said in unison as they all took a sip of champagne...

"Okay – let's eat!" Daddy said...

"Ryan?"

"Yes Cyn?"

"There's something we have to do first..."

"There is?"

"Yes..." Mommy answered as Chip came over to the table, pulled Mommy's chair into the middle of the room, took Mommy by the hand, and sat her down in the chair. Ryan stood there with a perplexed look on his face so the men started chanting to help him out...

"Take it off! Take it off! Take it off!"

"Oooohhh!" Daddy laughed and then he went over to Mommy and stood in front of her...

"Well?" Mommy asked...

"Ssshhh..." Daddy said as he bent down to kiss Mommy... and then he squatted down and pushed Mommy's legs open. Thank God Mommy's dress was long so nobody could see what was going on as he put his head up under her dress…

"Woo hoo!"

"Yea!"

"Take it off!" Daddy kissed his way up Mommy's thigh until he reached the garter and then he nibbled on her thigh as he took the garter in his teeth…

"Ryan… that tickles…" Mommy laughed as she grabbed his head…

"Save it for later!" Bri yelled out as everyone laughed and Daddy came out from under Mommy's dress with the garter in his teeth, stood up, and took a bow as everyone applauded. Daddy put the garter in his pocket, pulled Mommy up out the chair, and kissed her hard…

"Woo hoo!"

"Yea!" Robert came to get the chair and put it back at the table and waited for Mommy to sit down before they all got ready to eat….

"I need everybody to hold hands…" Daddy said. Daddy waited for everyone to hold hands and then he stood up, took Mommy's hand, and Robert's hand… "Lord – thank you – for everything!"

"Amen!" everyone said in unison. They all got up and went to the Buffet Station as jazz played in the background and they got the following:

Parmesan & Herb Panko Crusted Chicken with Garlic Sauce
Hand Rolled Beef Meatballs
Italian Sausage & Peppers
Baked Ziti with Mariana Sauce
Roasted Red Skinned Potatoes tossed with Olive Oil, Chopped Garlic & Fresh Parsley
Baked Eggplant Rollotini Tomato puree topped with sharp Provolone
Focaccia and Ciabatta bread with Butter

Cannoli Dip with Fresh Fruit and Crushed Cannoli Shells

Everyone ate until they were stuffed and then Daddy stood up..."Cyn?"

"Yes Ryan?"

"Come with me..." Daddy said as he extended his hand...

"Okay!" Mommy squealed as Daddy took Mommy over to the dessert...

"Smash it in his face! Smash it in his face!" everyone yelled...

"Ryan... I don't wanna..." Mommy said...

"Too late!" Daddy laughed as he took some Cannoli Dip off his off his plate and smashed it in Mommy's face as everyone laughed...

"Ryan! You got it in my hair!"

"I'm sorry..." he sighed...

"I'm not!" Mommy laughed as she took some Cannoli Dip and smashed it on the side of

Daddy's his face, making sure she got some of the cake and icing in his hair as everyone laughed…

"Come here Cyn…" he said as he smiled at her mischievously…

"No…" Mommy laughed…

"I said…" he laughed as he pulled Mommy close to him… "Come here… and open your mouth…" he laughed as he held a small piece of fruit in between his fingers…

"Okay… okay…" Mommy laughed as she opened her mouth and Daddy put the fruit in her mouth… "Mmmm… it's good… your turn…" Mommy said as she picked up a small piece of fruit in between her fingers and held it in front of Daddy's mouth…

"Okay… I'ma open my mouth… and you're not gonna smash it on my nose… right?"

"Ryan!"

"Okay…" he laughed as he opened his mouth and Mommy put a piece of fruit in his mouth…

"Mmmm…" he said as he pulled Mommy into a kiss and put his tongue in Mommy's mouth with fruit on it…

"Mmmm…" Mommy moaned…

"Y'all need us to leave?" Robert asked as everyone laughed…

"Y'all can stay if y'all want…" Daddy laughed as he picked up another piece of cake, held it between his lips, and pulled Mommy into another kiss…

"Aww shit!"

"Woo hoo!"

"C'mon – let's let everyone get dessert…" Daddy laughed as they went back to the table…

"I've never had dessert like that before…" Mommy laughed…

"Me either…"

"I wanna do it again…"

"We can." Everyone continued laughing, talking, eating, and drinking until it was time to go to their rooms...

"Okay – we're done – you'll have the pictures in a week..." the photographer said as his team packed up the equipment. Everyone went to their rooms and when Mommy and Daddy got in their room, Daddy pulled Mommy into a kiss...

"Are you ready to make love to your husband?"

"I'm ready..."

"Come with me..." Daddy said as he took Mommy by the hand and led her to the bed. Daddy helped Mommy out of her dress and Mommy helped Daddy unbutton his shirt. Once Mommy and Daddy were completely naked, they went to the top of the bed, pulled down the covers, and got in...

"Get on your back..." Mommy commanded. Daddy got on his back and I'm not sure what

Mommy was doing, but Daddy was moaning louder than usual...

"Cyn... Ooohhh... Yes..." Mommy was moving a little faster and Daddy continued moaning... "Ohhh... Cyn... Yeesss... Just like that..." Mommy kept moving and Daddy moaned really loud... "Cyn... I'm cumming... Cyn... Cyn... Cyn... UUUGGGHHHH!" After Daddy ejaculated I realized what was happening...

"Hiiii!" my brothers and sisters said as they sat at the bottom of Mommy's stomach on top of the food...

"Hiiii!" I beamed...

"Cyn... Cyn... Cyn..." Mommy was still doing whatever was making Daddy feel good and then she got up and sat down on Daddy and they both started moaning...

"Ryan... Ryan... Ryan..."

"Cyn... Cyn... Cyn..." Daddy grabbed Mommy's hips and pushed her back and forth and when he pushed himself up inside her, she moved back and forth and I felt like I was on a roller coaster...

"Oh Ryan... Ryan... Ryan... Yes..."

"Cyn... Cyn... Cyn... Huh..."

"Do it again Mommy! I laughed...

"Ryan... Don't stop... I'm cumming..."

"I'm cumming with you..."

"Aagh! Aagh! Aagh! Aagh! Aagh!"

"Uuugh! Uuugh! Uuugh! Uuugh! Uuugh!"

"That was fun Mommy!" I beamed. Mommy lay down on Daddy and they started kissing...

"You're a screamer..." Daddy breathed...

"I guess I am..." Mommy breathed...

"I love how you surprised me..."

"Was it good?"

"Hell hea..."

"I've wanted to do that to you ever since you did it to me..."

"Oh yea?"

"Yea..."

"I love you Mrs. Davis..."

"I love you too Mr. Davis..."

"We have to find a way to have sex quietly after our honeymoon – which reminds me..." Daddy said as he stopped kissing Mommy and sat up...

"Yes Ryan?" Mommy asked as she sat up next to Daddy...

"We're going to Hawaii – we're leaving on Wednesday..."

"Oh Ryan – I love you, I love you, I love you!" Mommy squealed as she kissed him all over his face and mouth...

"I love you too..." Daddy breathed as he pushed Mommy down on her back, spread her legs, and eased himself inside her again...

"Ryan... Oh Ryan... Ryan..." Daddy bent down to kiss Mommy and I moved back and forth with Mommy as she grabbed Daddy and pushed him inside her...

Mommy and Daddy are really happy. Mommy is 6 month's pregnant and I'm floating around in my embryotic fluid. Daddy got a job working at the Holloway Law Firm owned by Ally's parents so Mommy and Daddy were able to move out right after they got back from their honeymoon. Mommy and Daddy started taking classes online and Mommy was doing her homework when Daddy came in...

"Hi Honey – how was your day?"

"It was long without you..." Mommy said as she got up and went over to Daddy...

"Oh yea? Can I make it up to you?" Daddy asked as he led Mommy backwards into the bedroom...

"I dunno..."

"Le'me try... please..."

"Well..." Mommy breathed as Daddy took off her shirt and her bra... "Since you said please..."

"Mmmm..." Daddy said as he sucked Mommy's breast... "You're starting to get milk..."

"I know..." Mommy said as Daddy took her pants and panties off...

"Get on the bed..." Daddy said as he took off his shirt. Mommy got on the bed and watched Daddy take off his pants. Daddy couldn't get on top of Mommy anymore because I was growing so he got on the bed behind Mommy and eased himself inside her. Now that I'm bigger, every time Mommy and Daddy have sex I go swimming...

"Ryan... Ryan... Oh God... Ryan..."

"Cyn... Cyn... Cyn... Oh god... You feel so good..."

"Wee! Wee! Wee! Wee! Wee!" I laughed...